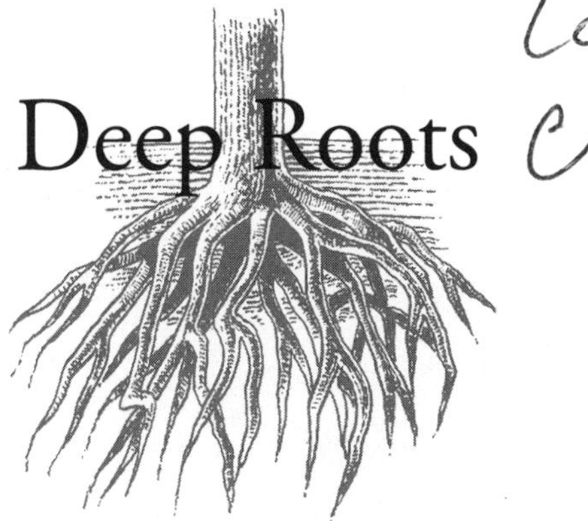

Deep Roots

Stories that Matter

Curt Iles

Author of
A Good Place and The Old House

Creekbank Stories

www.creekbank.net

Dedication

For my mother,
Mary Iles

"Curt, you can't have too many friends."
-My mom's lifelong advice.

Thanks for making me take Typing I. It's worked out well.

Dry Creek, LA USA
ISBN 978-0-9826492-1-3

Cover design by Chad Smith The Touch Studios www.thetouchstudios.com
Interior design by Marty Bee.

To order copies or contact the author:
Creekbank Stories
PO Box 332
Dry Creek, LA 70637
Toll free 1.866.520.1947
For corrections, input, and suggestions, email us at curtiles@aol.com
www.creekbank.net.
Join us at Face book and Twitter

Curt is represented by Terry Burns of Hartline Agency.
www. www.hartlineliterary.com

Titles by the author:
Deep Roots
A Good Place
The Wayfaring Stranger
The Mockingbird's Song
Hearts across the Water
Wind in the Pines
The Old House
Stories from the Creekbank

Available on audio CD:
Hearts across the Water
Wind in the Pines

Front Porch Stories

Acknowledgements

This book is a result of the encouragement of so many folks. At the risk of omitting names, I'd like to mention several who played key roles in bringing *Deep Roots* to print.

First, I thank my wife DeDe for her life-long support, love, and commitment.

My assistant Judi Reeves has been a breath of fresh air with her hard work, humor, and careful eye.

Sherry Perkins, Coleen Roberts Ritter, Joy Reeves Pitre, Julie Johnson, Colleen Glaser, Danny Woodall, Ashley Miller, and Lisa Buffaloe were great help on preparing this manuscript.

Marty Bee has once again proven himself a master with the beautiful interior design.

Chad Smith of The Touch Studios is a creative and talented artist who designed the cover of *Deep Roots*. His mother, Ruby Weldon Smith, gave the idea for the back cover design.

I'm grateful for the encouragement of John van Diest who prodded me to prepare this book.

Table of Contents

Title **Page**

CURT ILES

Deep Roots

Come to the woods, for here is rest.
-John Muir

The things that matter aren't really things.

It's because the things that matter in life are often unseen. They cannot be measured or placed in a bank account. Sometimes, they're even difficult to describe.

Like the deep roots of the tall trees of my beloved Louisiana woods, the things that matter are often deep and unseen. Yet, they give a lasting silent strength.

I recall a long ago trip to one of my favorite trees while hunting with my youngest son Terry. Leaving our deer stand in Crooked Bayou swamp, we made a detour to this special spot.

We arrived at a huge beech tree, surrounded by fallen dead limbs. This old tree was dying, as evidenced by its bare trunk and remaining leafless limbs. This was my first visit this hunting season, and I was shocked at how the tree deteriorated. I wondered if this was the mighty tree's final year.

I pointed out to Terry what made this beech tree so special. Carved about four feet high was:

F.I.
L.I.
10/9/21

"F.I." was my great-grandfather, Frank Iles, and "L.I." was my grandfather, Lloyd Iles. On a hunting trip of their own over seventy-six years ago, they had carved their initials on this tree. On that Friday in 1921, my great-grandfather was thirty-six, his son was ten, and the tree was already old. It was the queen of the swamp.

However, soon it will be gone.

On this day, my son and I were close to the respective ages of my beloved ancestors. A sense of deep roots overwhelmed me. It was a special moment with my son as we stood on land that had been in our family since the nineteenth century.

Another emotion also overwhelmed me—the feeling of how quickly life comes and goes. Each time I've stood at this tree, I'm reminded of the certainty of life passing right before our eyes.

Yes, time passes by so quickly—and life's limbs fall to the ground as sure as the cold November wind blows. What precious gifts we have been given—this gift of life, the wonderful gift of family—both past and present, and for me, the gift of an old beech tree deep in Crooked Bayou swamp. A family tree with deep roots.

A reminder of the things that really matter.
So come into the woods with me for these stories.
Stories of family, faith, and friends.
Stories from the woods, as well as stories of the woods.
Stories of the deep-rooted things that really matter.

Curt Iles
Dry Creek, Louisiana
November 2010

The Landmark Pine

It's the lone pine tree featured on the front cover of this book. It's a landmark tree, a special type of tree tied to the history of our area.

The early pioneers used these trees as waypoints for wagon trains and travelers.

The landmark pine on the cover of *Deep Roots* is along the Longville-Dry Creek Road, commonly called the "Gravel Pit Road." It's a winding eleven-mile track that has only recently been paved.

I love traveling this road because most of it is pine woods bisected by three creek crossings: Dry Creek (twice) and Barnes Creek. Due to the seclusion of the road, it is prime territory for spotting wild turkey and deer.

Before we drive from Dry Creek to the Landmark Tree, it's time for a short lesson.

The early settlers in America knew about landmark trees. A good example of this is the community of Lone Tree, Iowa. It derives its name from a giant elm that grew nearby in the pioneer era. It was the only prairie landmark between the Iowa and Cedar Rivers.

It was a defining point in that area until its death from Dutch Elm Disease in the 1960s.

In Piney Woods Louisiana, the timber clear cuts of the early twentieth century left only a few pines standing. These trees naturally became useful as landmarks for travelers as in, "The road turns left over thar just past that big pine."

Traveling west from Dry Creek toward the Landmark Tree, you pass two of the finest preserved dogtrot houses in

Louisiana: the Fanny Heard house, followed by the Mary Jane Lindsey home place.

Just south of the Lindsey home is where my first Dry Creek ancestors homesteaded in 1848. Andrew Jackson Wagnon and Nancy Fulton Wagnon traveled from Georgia to stake their claim in the No Man's Land. They homesteaded in the edge of Dry Creek Swamp near a free-flowing spring.

A few years ago I walked the entire Gravel Pit Road. As I walked over the hill and down toward the swamp, I was overwhelmed that this was probably the same path A.J. Wagnon walked when he left for the Civil War.

He never returned, dying near Opelousas, Louisiana of Typhoid Fever. His wife Nancy lived on the homestead until her death nearly forty years later. The Wagnon descendants are scattered all over the Piney Woods.

Continuing toward the Landmark Tree, we pass the site of the one-room Mt. Moriah School. It's where my ancestors walked to school during the nineteenth century. I have a photo of the thirty-member student body gathered in front of the one-room school. It was nicknamed the "Hen Scratch School" due to chickens scratching around the yard where the students ate their lunches.

The Landmark Tree stands on the north side of the bumpy road as we enter the secluded part of the trip. We'll stop by it and talk more on the return trip.

After crossing Dry Creek the second time, we pass over Grave's Gully. If you walk south along it, you'll come to the Jayhawker graves.

Two local men, William Washington Green and Lemuel Jackson Bradford, were ambushed and murdered by jayhawkers in 1865. This spot is a reminder that our area's nickname of "The Outlaw Strip" was well-deserved. Even now a visit to the two lone graves has an eerie feel to it.

To the north of the main road is the abandoned gravel pit. For a generation, truck after truck of gravel and pebbles were mined from the pit. I remember my father trying to get

Wildlife and Fisheries to stop the gravel pit from dumping its wastewater into Dry Creek.

It was my first time to understand about conservation, stewardship, and a love of the land. Although his campaign was unsuccessful, I'll always admire Dad's stand.

Soon the traveler crosses over Barnes Creek, still thirty winding miles from its junction with the Calcasieu River. Looking at the creek now, it's hard to fathom how log rafts were once floated to the sawmills on Lake Charles.

Closer to Barnes Creek's mouth is where another branch of my family arrived in the early 1800s. Most of them are buried at one of Louisiana's most beautiful graveyards, Lyles Cemetery, between Bel and Topsy.

The Gravel Pit Road climbs out of the swamp and back into the pines as it nears the once thriving sawmill town of Longville. Long Bel Lumber from Longview, Washington operated a large mill during the cutting of the virgin pine forests that had stood for hundreds of years.

In the "cut out/clear out" philosophy of the times, all of the pines were cut. Very few landmark trees were left.

Let's double back and stop for a talk under the Landmark Tree.

Another name for these lone trees were "seed trees." These were trees spared during the lumbering for the purpose of providing a source of seed for re-stocking the over-cut areas.

The longleaf pine has huge cones which contain the small seeds that can grow into trees. Sadly, very few were left. The result was a stump-filled expanse of grassy land. My great-grandfather, Frank Iles, told of walking from Dry Creek to Reeves and being able to see for miles. He told of constantly being on the lookout for wild bulls due to the lack of trees to climb for escape.

Another name for the lone trees left behind is "witness trees." As the original public land surveys were done in the early 1800's, every section and quarter section were marked by nearby witness trees.

My father was a land surveyor. In seeking the corners of land parcels, he'd look for the witness trees. They normally had a large X cut into the bark with an ax. I've seen Daddy dig futilely for the stump of a long gone witness tree needed to clearly mark a corner.

ꟃ

There's an additional meaning of witness tree. It refers to an old tree that witnessed a historic event and still stands as a silent testimony.

The Gettysburg Battlefield is a hallowed spot for all Americans. On Culp's Hill where the Union fortifications helped ensure victory over the Confederates stands a witness tree.

It was there during the fierce three days of battle in July 1863. A few weeks later, famed photographer Matthew Brady took a photograph showing two of his assistants sitting on a rock by the tree.

That tree still stands today as a witness to how our nation's history hung in the balance. It's a witness tree of history. Our American history.

My research led to other stories of landmark and witness trees. In cases of famous trees toppling in a storm or from old age, it was reported as if a death in the family had occured. The passing of a landmark tree calls for mourning.

I wonder if I'll see the demise of the Gravel Pit Road tree. It looks pretty sturdy. I hope it outlasts me. I also hope to one day take a great-grandchild to see the tree.

It has rode out several strong hurricanes in 1918, 1957, and 2005. In the photo you can see where it lost a limb on the left during Hurricane Rita.

It's a large landmark tree with strong roots. As this book went to print, my son Clint measured its diameter at 29 inches. He took out his increment bore and drilled into its core. He estimated its age at least seventy-five years, maybe more. As I examined the pencil-sized core, the sweet aroma of pine sap filled the truck cab.

It's a worthy landmark tree, but it's not the Louisiana Landmark Tree. That designation belongs to the twenty-eight live oaks forming the entrance to Oak Alley Plantation along the Mississippi River. They predate the 1718 founding of New Orleans and are majestic to see.

Don't tell the folks at Oak Alley, but I wouldn't trade a hundred live oaks for the Dry Creek Landmark Pine. It marks the area that I call home. That's why I wanted it on the cover of *Deep Roots*.

It marks a spot. A spot that my heart calls home.

It's also a seed tree.

During its long fruitful life, it's provided seeds and pollen for new trees in the surrounding area. Younger trees have been grown, thinned, cut, replanted, and cut again. All that time, the landmark tree has watched in its place of honor along the old fencerow.

I guess it's kind of like a proud grandpa or great grandpa. It's survived the axes, crosscut saws, chain saws, and hydraulic shears of generations of Louisiana timber men.

It's a witness tree. A reminder of the legacy of the longleaf pine that defines western Louisiana. Our economy, our culture, even our philosophy, is tied to this tree.

A landmark pine standing proudly alone in the heart of Beauregard Parish, Louisiana.

Long may it stand.

Burned yet Blessed

"The best time to plant a tree is twenty years ago. The next best time is today."

Nothing breaks my heart like a field of burned pines. Yet that is exactly what I'm looking at driving toward the community of Reeves, Louisiana—forty acres of longleaf pines have been the victim of a forest fire.

This must have been an extremely hot fire. It completely burned the smaller trees and blackened the bark of the more mature trees. It's sad seeing acres of pines with burnt trunks and brown straw. It appears the entire stand will need to be replanted.

These trees might look dead but they aren't. There is an amazing story behind the burning and growth of *Pinus palustrus*, the Southern Longleaf Pine. This native tree, also called the yellow pine, ruled the virgin forests from Virginia to East Texas. Because of its hardiness and adaptability in growing in shallow, sandy soils, it covered much of the acreage of the southern United States

These beautiful pines existed in vast tracts called pine savannahs, upland areas where the pines were scattered throughout grassy areas. Fire was always a reality in dry weather and after the killing frosts of winter.

The native Indians first burned the woods so they could better see game animals and lessen the chance of their enemies hiding nearby. Later, white settlers burned these same grasslands for better grazing for their cattle and sheep, as well as killing pests such as redbugs and ticks.

No matter the reason for these fires, the longleaf pines

could survive the heat. In fact, fire is imperative for the early development and growth of this species.

The early stage of a longleaf pine is called the grassy stage. The tree has hardly any trunk above ground and the long green needles more nearly resemble a wild type of grass than a tree. The pine will stay in this stage indefinitely—unless a fire sweeps through.

Tremendous growth is taking place underground. The small visible tree is sending down a strong taproot, that anchors it deeply into the earth and stores energy and nutrients for its future.

During this grassy stage, the visible tree will remain dormant due to what is called Brown Spot Needle Blight. This fungus attacks the topmost growth area of the young pine, called the candle bulb.

This combination of the tall grass competing with the seedlings for sunshine and nutrients, plus the Needle Blight, keeps the young tree from growing upward. The surrounding grass keeps the area moist, which is the condition the Needle Blight needs to attack the small pine's candle bulb. The result is that the longleaf sapling will remain alive, but never grow upward.

This species will never reach its potential until a fire rushes through, killing the grass and other competing trees. Additionally, the heat of the fire kills the Brown Spot Needle Blight. The bushy longleaf pine is now freed for growth to its intended height.

I love the resilience of these trees. Looking across the tract along the Reeves Highway, blackened and charred pines stretch endlessly. In spite of their appearance, I know these burned trees are still alive.

In the succeeding weeks, I watch the field for new growth. In March, the trees begin their miracle with new green sprouting. Soon new healthy candle bulbs, some nearly a foot long, begin reaching upwards. Over the coming weeks and months, these thin bulbs turn into tree trunks and sprout fresh pine straw. These longleaf seedlings, once dwarfed by the grass and bushes, will never again compete for water, sunlight, or food.

Knowing about this species, I also know that this same growth is taking place underground. During the grassy stage, the underground taproot is growing strong and deep, giving it a stable foundation for its upward journey.

There's a spiritual application from the story of the longleafs. In our lives, the fire of trials grow us into the person God wants us to be. None of us desire these times of heat and pain, but God uses them for the shaping of our taproot—the heart—for maximum growth.

We see a memorable example of this "burned yet blessed" experience in the Old Testament story of Shadrach, Meshach, and Abednego. The book of Daniel tells of these three young men being thrown into the fiery furnace for refusing to bow to the Babylonian King Nebuchadnezzar.

Our three heroes were thrown in tightly bound, as good as dead. The fire was so hot that it killed the soldiers tossing them in this furnace. In a few minutes the King was amazed to see them walking around in the fire. Daniel 3:25 tells of his reaction.

"Look!" he answered, "I see four men loose, walking in the midst of the fire; and they are not hurt, and the form of the fourth is like the Son of God."

God did not desert them but personally showed up and stood by them. In this fire, what bound them, the ropes, were burned off. Just like the longleaf's fungus blight, the hot fire destroyed what was holding them back.

We all experience being in the fire at various times in our lives. None of us is exempt. Your fire will probably be much different from mine. Regardless, God wishes to use this fire for shaping and using you. Throughout history, the people God has most used have been those who've worked through difficult circumstances and grown to their maximum height for use by Him.

When you are in the fire, remember that God has not abandoned you. Just as God joined Shadrach and his two partners in the Babylonian fire, you are not alone. Your faithful Father is using this fiery trial to shape you for optimum use by Him.

If you are ever driving along La. 113 between Reeves and Dry Creek, look west at about mile marker 3. You'll see a field of longleaf pines of all sizes. Some are in neat rows while others have come up on their own.

The hot fire has burned in these pines. They're burned yearly to help them grow. What looks like a terrible thing is truly a blessing.

These trees tell a memorable story.

The story of deep roots, thick bark, and a lasting resilience.

Longleaf pines that have been burned—yet blessed—by the fire.

"A fellow is in one of three places in his life: coming from a fire, going toward a fire, or in the midst of a fire. There's one common denominator: God stands by us in each one."

The Door

This is a warning: Be careful with the doors at the Lake Charles Civic Center! I was there last week and as I entered the men's room, I recalled Roy Greene's story.

The Lake Charles Civic Center opened thirty years ago. It was constructed on sand pumped out of the adjacent lake that gives the city of Lake Charles its name.

In keeping with the French heritage of our area, it was christened "Le Civic Centre." In carrying out this Acadian motif, the restrooms were labeled as "Messieurs" and "Madames."

The thoughtful architect also designed the "Messieurs/ Madames" restrooms so there was one entrance door (with no handle on the inside) and a corresponding exit door on the other end. This wisely (or unwisely as our story will reveal) ensured that users all moved in one direction.

And that brings us to Roy Greene's famous story. Mr. Roy, a Dry Creek native, loved basketball. He had played on Dry Creek High's famous undefeated 1931 state championship team, coached high school ball, and was the long time principal at Fenton High. He produced a line of great coaches including his son, Larry, and grandsons Mike and Chris Greene.

Mr. Roy loved the Sweet 16 State Girl's Basketball Tournament, and never missed a game. On this particular year, it was held at the Lake Charles Civic Center. During a halftime break, Mr. Roy, who was near eighty, shuffled to the restroom, hurrying so as not to miss a minute of action on the court.

Maybe it was his eyesight, or his preoccupation with the game—

When he got to the door, he thought it was "Messieurs" but (I know you are ahead of me) instead, it was "Madames." Mr. Roy did not realize his mistake until he was inside and saw two sobering sights: no urinals and a restroom full of women.

Of course, he did what any man would do: he discreetly retreated to the entrance door. However, there was no handle. He stood not quite sure what to do … and then did the only thing he knew to do—he shuffled along right through the restroom, parting the throng of startled women, and then out the exit door.

His son Larry, who watched from the lobby, said, "I saw him go in the wrong door and tried to catch him, but I was too late. When he came out the other end, I told him, 'You ain't nothing but a dirty old man'!"

Last week as I entered the Civic Center's "Messieurs" restroom, I did a double take just to make sure. I laughed at the corresponding "Men" sign below the "Messieurs."

Probably put there in memory of my friend, Mr. Roy Greene.

If you're familiar with my writing, you know how I like to find a spiritual meaning in my stories. Well, here goes: it's about making good decisions, i.e. "going through the right doors."

Life is a series of many decisions, most small, others huge, but all propelling us in a definite direction. We don't get where we are by accident, but by a series of decisions.

Realistically, many choices, like Mr. Roy's Door, offer no retreat. Therefore, we want to select the correct doors leading into the right places.

Yesterday, I read one of my life verses, "Trust in the Lord with all your heart, and lean not on your own understanding. In all your ways acknowledge Him, and He shall direct your paths." Proverbs 3:5-6

In my simple Dry Creek mind that means if I trust God, listen to him, and include him in my decisions, he will help me choose the right doors. That verse is a promise, and it is a promise for you too!

Have a great day, Messieurs and Madames!

The Pine Knot Pile

Suddenly, the February wind picked up and turned out of the south. Instantly what had been a small controlled fire in my back field morphed into a raging monster.

The flames spread rapidly through the dead knee high grass—as fast I as I could, I ran ahead with my faithful firefighting weapon—a wet grass sack. But no one person, nor any wet sack, was going to curtail this fire. It had a malicious mind of its own as it raced northward.

DeDe and the boys came running out of the house. Armed with brooms, buckets, and a shovel, they ran to join me but we were all driven back by the racing fire. We watched as the fire sped toward one of my most precious possessions: my pine knot pile.

Before returning to this fire, let me clue you in on what a pine knot pile is. Southwestern Louisiana was naturally populated with yellow pines, or as we now call them, longleaf pines. Every area of upland was covered with these slow-growing but stately pines. During the late 19th and early 20th centuries, all of the virgin pine forests were clear-cut by large timber companies. Where huge tracts of pines had once towered, only open fields of stumps now stood. The timber companies cleared large areas, then moved on.

These Yellow Pines had many great qualities. Prime among them was the tree's large heart, or inner core. This resiny heart, instead of rotting, turned into a rich, sappy wood. These remains of pine stumps were called "rich lighter" or "fat pine."

Due to its thick resin, lighter pine would burn easily and

for generations were the preferred method of starting fires in cook stoves and fireplaces.

In the 1940's, Crosby Chemical Company of Picayune, Mississippi moved into Beauregard Parish and began harvesting the remaining stumps for their turpentine mill. Turpentine, the syrupy resin in pine stumps, has many commercial purposes.

Country people gathered all of the rich pine they could for their personal use. Every older home had a large pine pile.

Settlers considered their pine supply a great prize. Fires were the method of keeping warm and cooking. During the winter a fire was usually burning in either the fireplace or cook stove around the clock.

Over the years as propane and electricity became part of our rural culture, cook stoves and cooking in the fireplace became lost arts.

In spite of these modern improvements, most people kept their fireplaces going. There is no substitute for sitting cozily by a popping and crackling fire as the cold wind moans and the rain blows against the house.

When DeDe and I bought our Dry Creek home in 1985, I was excited about inheriting an ample pine knot pile in the corner of our back field. The land on which we now live had been a second growth forest until it was cleared for soybean farming in the 1960's.

As they cleared the land I now live on, the pine stumps and knots were stacked in an impressive pile in the corner of the field. It was head high and twenty feet wide.

With pride I pointed my treasure out to family and friends. I could feel the envy of men as they coveted my pine pile. There was enough here to easily last a lifetime and more.

I tried not to be completely selfish with this abundant supply. I shared wheelbarrow loads with my dad, family, and neighbors. Even after ten years of use, I hadn't even made a good dent in my pine pile.

This hot runaway fire in my back field—started by me—is

approaching my pine knot pile, and was going to make more than a dent in it. As soon as the brush fire touched the pine pile, it was engulfed in flames. The fire and thick choking black smoke billowed high into the sky.

If it'd been anything but my pine knot pile, watching this would have been enjoyable . . . but it was my lifetime supply of pine literally going up in smoke as we stood and watched helplessly.

DeDe went inside and contacted the the fire tower as to the source of the billowing black smoke. The tower observer replied, "Ma'am, go easy on your husband. It's a tough thing on a man to lose his pine knot pile."

It had all happened so quickly and was over in a matter of minutes. Where fifteen minutes earlier my huge pine knot pile had towered, was now only charred ashes and smoking chunks of wood.

When I read Jesus' words in Matthew, I envision my precious pine knot pile. He reminds us that all earthly treasures someday will rust, corrode, rot, become moth-eaten, be discarded and abandoned, or as in my case—burn up.

When you see someone driving a new car off the sales lot, remember that one day the new and shiny car, will be junked, smashed, and melted down.

Jesus told us to hoard Heavenly treasures – the things that really last: eternal things. The only things I've seen that really last are God's word, His love, and people's souls. Therefore, that's where our treasures should be.

Earthly treasures have their place, but we should never forget they are only temporary. Just like my pine knot pile, they can quickly and unexpectedly leave us. The things of God are the only things that really matter—and they last forever.

"Do not store up for yourselves treasures on earth, where moth and rust destroy, and where thieves break in and steal. But store up for yourselves treasures in heaven, where moth and rust do not destroy, and where thieves do not break in and steal. For where your treasure is, there will your heart be also."

Matthew 6: 20-21

Tough or Hard

In front of me are three objects: a brick, a piece of leather, and a hammer. These make for a wonderful lesson.

However, this story is not about the hardness of a brick, toughness of leather, or the pain of the hammer blow. This is a story about somebody. Objects don't move us—but people do.

Watching folks go through difficult times is revealing. Periods of trial and adversity serve to distill what is really inside people. What's revealed often surprises and shocks us.

Hurricanes Katrina and Rita did that for us in Louisiana. The whole world saw the worst side of humans—you saw it on the television with the looting, abandonment and loss in New Orleans.

Then again, this storm blew in and exposed the best sides of humankind. Strangers reaching across all sorts of lines—racial, cultural, or geographical—to help others in need.

Observing it, I was amazed watching how our storms, and the ensuing difficulties that followed, elicited completely different responses in people. Some folks, comfortable living their lives as victims, continued blaming the world for their troubles. Others in exactly the same circumstances quickly got back up, dusted themselves off and went to work, choosing to be a victor instead of a victim.

The human spirit and corresponding attitudes are amazing to observe. It comes down to this: Life will make you either hard or tough.

You become either bitter . . . or better.

ꟷ

Let's look at our three objects: the brick, the hammer, and the strip of leather. Place the piece of leather and the brick on a sidewalk side by side. Now, take the hammer and hit each one of them hard several times. The brick will be broken into pieces. The piece of leather may show the hammer's indents, but it will not break or crack.

Because bricks are hard, but leather is tough.

What happens to us—it's called circumstances—will make us either hard or tough. These situations are the hammer blows. It doesn't matter whether the blows are self-inflicted or due to chance or fate. They may be due to family circumstances, what we call rotten luck, a cancer diagnosis, or a hurricane:

The sources of life's hammer blows are limitless.

These blows come to all of us. No one is immune.

Some people will become tougher when the hammer falls. They take the blows, their lives showing the imprints of the hammer, but they are supple and flexible. They come out of this experience tougher and still whole.

Under the same circumstances others, like the brick, crack and crumble under the same blows. That is because like the brick, they have become hard.

Sadly, hardness does not ensure toughness. There are hard-to-miss traits that exemplify hardness in life: bitterness, an attitude of apathy toward the needs and pain of others, or a selfish callousness that strives to isolate oneself from the world. Add to this list, the telltale symptom of cynicism toward others, God, and spiritual things.

Under the hammer blows of life—who we are, as well as what we really believe—will always be revealed.

Here's a good question: How do you recognize a tough heart? The short letter below explains the tough heart. It's from my aptly named friend: Joy Tanner:

2005 was a tumultuous year of storms for Jack and me; the fiery fatal plane crash in which our daughter lost her life; the people with whom we spent twenty years in Cameron Parish who lost it all because of Hurricane Rita; the news that our deceased daughter's only child is going to Iraq; my husband Jack's Lou Gehrig's disease.

In spite of the great losses, we've become better instead of bitter. It's a peace that comes from the inside, from inside the heart where the mold cannot grow.

And the water cannot flood.

And the hurricane-force winds cannot reach.

And the flames of the plane crash cannot burn up.

Amen and amen,

Joy Tanner

Her letter reveals the heart of a brave and tough woman who has not allowed her spirit to be hard.

Her name—Joy—says it all.

Joy—unlike happiness—comes from inside and cannot be taken away by situations, storms, even tragedies.

Joy Tanner was hammered repeatedly in 2005, but she came out of it better, not bitter.

Tough, not hard.

Tough as leather, more useful and usable for God—as well as to others.

Tough, but not hard.

May the same be said of each of us.

C U R T   I L E S

Branded

"He who guards his mouth and his tongue keeps himself from calamity."
-Proverbs 21:23

The fight on MacArthur Drive was one-sided, and although it was over quickly, it's never been forgotten.

To truly appreciate Donald Perkins' famous lop-sided 1970 scuffle in the middle of MacArthur Drive's four lanes, you must understand where he came from.

The place is called Pitkin.

Pitkin. I've always liked the way it rolls off your tongue. They say it there with two strong syllables, as in "Pit-Kin."

Calling it a town is a gross exaggeration. It's a village—it's really not even that—just a caution light, several stores and churches. It's full of good people who would do anything if you're in need. It also has a well-known reputation for being a tough place. There is a saying about Pitkin people, "They're the best friends you'd ever want, but the worst enemies you could ever have."

There are many stories about Pitkin and its people, but none better than the one I call "Branded."

Now, Donald Perkins was a Pitkin native who operated the DeRidder Sale Barn, where weekly cattle auctions took place. Tuesday was sale day and the barn would be crowded with trucks, trailers, cowboys, mooing cows, bleating sheep, in the middle of this dusty scene stood Donald Perkins.

On the day of my "Branded" story, Donald Perkins wasn't at the sale barn. He was traveling through the city of

Alexandria with a load of cattle. He wore his cowboy hat, and had the truck window rolled down. Tapping his brakes, he brought his rig to a stop at a red light on Alexandria's main street, MacArthur Drive.

A car in the adjacent left lane joined him. It was a Muscle Car: a Dodge Charger. Fueled by a large V-8 engine, it was loud, powerful, and ready to roll.

This particular red Dodge had four occupants—longhaired hippies with scruffy beards and sloppy clothes. They sneered as they pulled up beside the cattle truck.

Two distinct cultures were meeting side by side on the pavement of MacArthur Drive. Because there were four of them, the hippies bravely began making fun of the short red-faced cowboy beside them. Their comments were low, but Donald Perkins heard enough—he knew they were making fun of him, his truck, and his load.

Fortunately, the light turned green and the Dodge Charger, with its loud glass-packed dual exhausts, roared away. Donald and his loaded truck took off much slower.

As fate would have it, the next red light caught both vehicles. As you can probably guess, they were once again side by side. They arrived there ahead of the cattle truck, so the four hippies had plenty of time getting their one-line zingers ready for the cowboy. They directed their sarcastic remarks straight at Donald Perkins.

As I told you earlier, men from the Pitkin area are not the enemies you want. It was when they made a remark about his load of cows and directed it at him, that Donald had heard enough. Today we would call what he did next "road rage," but that term had not been coined yet in 1970.

He calmly killed his engine—and reached back behind him on his gun rack and pulled down a weapon.

But it wasn't a shotgun or rifle … instead, it was something even better: a cattle prod … or what we call a "hotshot."

This tool is a thin pole about the size of a walking stick.

On the business end protrudes two metal electrodes. When it is shoved against a conductive object, it gives a sharp jolt of electricity.

The hotshot is a prime tool for any serious cattleman. It is effective in controlling even the most stubborn bull. The shock doesn't cause long-term damage, but quickly and completely gets the attention of even the most onery animal.

Now I know you are ahead of me on my story, so let's get back to the scene. Donald Perkins jumped out of his truck, quickly approaching the carload of "rowdy animals" just as if he was back on the sale barn's show floor.

The guy on the front passenger side was wearing a sleeveless shirt with his arm propped up on the door. His sneer changed as Donald stuck him in the armpit. He later said of the first guy, "That fellow bleated like a goat."

In quick succession, he stuck all of them. With all of the hollering, cussing, and scampering around he couldn't be sure, but Donald thought he got the two on the passenger side a couple of extra times for good measure.

The Charger was fenced in on all sides, so they couldn't drive off. Finally, the light turned green, the cars ahead moved off, and the hippies in the Dodge roared off, probably not slowing down until they got across the Red River and into Pineville.

I have told and retold this story hundreds of times since the day Donald's nephew "T-Bone" Perkins first acted it out in detail for me.

Donald Perkins has now been dead for many years, but in my mind he is still alive—standing in the traffic lane of busy MacArthur Drive wielding his weapon like a skilled swordsman through the open windows of the hippie car.

. . . And probably somewhere in Rapides Parish, or maybe up in Pollock . . . or down in Bunkie, some fifty-something-year old guy will read this story . . . and feel a twinge of remembrance. Maybe the twinge will be felt under his right arm, or a jolt in his memory, as he remembers that day on the four lane in Alexandria—when the crazy cowboy attacked him and his buddies.

Yes, that day will be forever "branded" in his mind—a day when he was stuck by the short cowboy from Pitkin… That's Pitkin, Louisiana, boy … And when you say it, say it with respect. Where the men are strong, the women are beautiful, and you don't make fun of a man's cowboy hat, his truck, or his load of cows.

Most of my stories have some spiritual lesson. I'm not sure about this one. I guess it's a lesson on keeping your mouth shut and minding your own business, especially if you're parked next to a cowboy with a loaded gun rack.

I love the book of Proverbs and try reading one chapter daily.* Solomon and the other writers impart much practical and common sense wisdom in its thirty-one chapters. It says, "Even a fool is thought to be wise if he keeps silent." (Proverbs 17:28) That's a lesson the four hippies hopefully learned. Or as my Uncle Quincy, who spent two tours of duty at Angola Prison, said, "They ain't never sent nobody to the pen for keeping their mouth shut."

Or as Solomon added in Proverbs, "When words are many, sin is not absent, but he who holds his tongue is wise."

Keeping your mouth shut—a good lesson that should be branded into our minds. Be careful what you say and whom you say it to, especially if a cowboy is in the lane next to you.

Or as they say in Pitkinese, "If you ain't got somethin' good to say, keep it to yerself."

Even King Solomon couldn't say it better than that.

** A Bible reading plan I adopted years ago is called the "Daily Proverbs Plan." Because Proverbs consists of 31 chapters, you can read the corresponding chapter on that day of the month. Proverbs is full of so much wisdom that re-reading it monthly never gets old.*

The Evening Holler

The call of two owls deep in Crooked Bayou Swamp at daybreak takes me back to a story told by my great-grandmother.

It's before daybreak on a cool still October morning. During this month, Louisiana begins cooling off, and most of the month features clear skies and lower humidity.

As first light approaches, a neighbor's rooster crows a mile through the woods. In the opposite direction, I hear a distant dog barking non-stop. Early mornings—deep in the woods—always amaze me with how sounds carry so clearly and distinctly. There is a clarity and crispness to early morning sounds that stir the soul.

First, the rooster—then the dog—each take a break and the returning silence of the swamp covers me like a warm blanket. A nearby owl with his eight-note song eventually breaks this calm. Soon another sentry joins him across the swamp. These two barred owls converse back and forth in their unique eight-note call:

"Hoo hoo-hoo hoo—hoo hoo-hoo hoawww."

When hearing their calls, I recall old-timers describing it as,

"Who cooks for you? Who cooks for you-all?"

We Southerners always comment that the barred owl's ending "you-all" proves he is also one of us.

Even knowing it's owls, there's a mystery in their cries echoing now through the dark swamp. The owl's conversation draws me back to my favorite story about the settling of our community. I call it "The Evening Holler."

It's a story I'd like to pass on to you.

My great grandparents told this tale of the evening holler. This unique call, a tradition going back to the pre-Civil War settling of our area, provided primitive communication among the early settlers.

The first non-Indian settlers in Dry Creek lived in the woods along the winding creeks and streams. Vast tracts of uninhabited pine forests surrounded these pioneers. This area of Southwestern Louisiana was a neutral strip claimed by both Spain and the United States. Initially, no law existed, and even later, the nearest officer was over seventy miles away. Indians—though reasonably friendly—still roamed the woods, while bears and mountain lions were common in the swamps.

Because these pioneers homesteaded large tracts of land, they seldom built homes right next to each other. By necessity, they depended on each other, so they developed an ingenious method of checking on the welfare of their neighbors.

Late in the evening at dusk, each man stood on the porch of his home. Just as the sun dropped behind the wooded horizon, the ritual began. Each of the pioneers had his own unique hollering style—easily recognized by his own pitch and voice. The closest settler answered back, followed by the next one down the creek. As the evening holler passed back and forth through the woods, each man knew of his neighbor's well-being.

In this time, there were few artificial noises—this was long before televisions, air conditioners, airplanes, or vehicles—drowning out the sounds of nature and silence.

If a man didn't hear his neighbor's call, he'd wait a few minutes before hollering again. If repeating brought no reply, he'd go check on the next homestead. My great-grandmother told of seeing her father ride his horse over to check on a neighbor who hadn't answered. Even though things would usually be fine at the homestead, he went each time to look-in-on them. It was simply a matter of "being neighborly." The defining mark of these early settlers was that they looked after one another.

I guess you could say "The Evening Holler" was kind of an early version of today's "Neighborhood Watch." They truly considered a neighbor just that—a neighbor, someone to look after, and look out for.

In our present day busy lives, we seldom know our neighbors— and often neglect checking on their well-being. Even with all of our marvelous modern communication tools—from telephones to fax machines to e-mail—we usually know much less about those "next door" than our ancestors did.

After my morning in the woods, I'm back at home. Sitting on the front porch, I think about our contemporary lives, and how much we've lost in basic "neighborliness." On the highway, a horn honks and startles me from these thoughts. My neighbor, known to everyone as "Uncle Joe," drives by in his truck. He's seen me sitting here and his honk acknowledges that fact. I guess in its own way, his honk is a modern version of the evening holler.

Uncle Joe's truck is loaded down with firewood. The cool weather has made folks eager to use their fireplaces. There's something I know about Uncle Joe: he doesn't even have a fireplace anymore. His wife Mary sealed it up after it kept sooting up the house.

Regardless, he cuts firewood all fall and into winter for the widows of the community. As his truck disappears around the curve, I'm reminded: maybe the "evening holler" isn't as dead as I thought it was.

Thinking of each of these, and countless other kind deeds, I'm reminded how much goodness still exists in people. Yes, times have changed, but there is still plenty of "neighborliness" floating around. We don't live in as close contact with our neighbors as we once did—or even as we should.

As humans, we should take ownership on caring for those around us—"our community." It's a decision that each of us can do—and a positive decision that many of my neighbors have chosen to make. A simple—but powerful—decision on being "neighborly."

These neighbors—these lifetime friends—who remind me that the spirit of "The Evening Holler" is alive and well in a small community I love called Dry Creek.

Postscript

It's been my privilege to recently travel to Africa five times. The purpose of these trips has been to positively share the gospel of Jesus Christ through the building of relationships and sharing stories.

I've found that my rural-flavored stories translate well into the culture of the African people. Folks love a good story the world over.

I told the story you've just read, "The Evening Holler," during our visit to the former township of Sweetwaters in Zululand, South Africa.

As usual, I told "Evening Holler" using my mimics of the barred owl's calls.

A week later, we returned to the same area. A group of Zulu boys ran up, giving the Piney Woods Hoot Owl Call. As they did an encore at my request, I shot the photo on the back cover. Amazingly, these boys had the tone and sound of the owl down pat. I hope they understood the purpose of the story as well as they did the call.

The power of a story. It's understood in every language and culture.

"The shortest distance between a heart and the truth is a story."
-Anthony deMello

Across the Pea Patch

I often write about traveling to far off places sharing the good news of Jesus. Whether it's Africa or Honduras, I feel privileged to "go and tell."

Acts 1:8 tells us to "go to the ends of the earth." In the same verse Jesus calls our home "Jerusalem." This is where the greatest missions and ministry opportunities are.

It's the place we are.

Where we live.

Where we already know the culture, don't have to learn a new language, get immunizations, or apply for a passport.

I was reminded of this today as I talked to Don Hunt. He is one of the people I admire most.

He was my pastor for ten years.

He is my friend.

He's also one of my heroes.

This is my favorite Don Hunt story. It's a "Jerusalem" story, and in this case, Jerusalem is a Dry Creek purple hull pea patch.

When he became our pastor in 1992, he began doing what he does best: building relationships. After he'd been in Dry Creek for a few weeks, he walked across the adjacent field to meet his next-door neighbor, Arthur Crow.

Mr. Arthur's wife, Annie Mae, was already a member of our congregation at Dry Creek Baptist Church. Mr. Arthur, now retired from driving the road grader for the police jury, was not a church-going man. He was a good man, but seemingly had no interest in church or outward spiritual things.

When Bro. Don walked over, Mrs. Annie Mae directed him to the pea patch where her husband was working. Don

Hunt introduced himself and they visited as Mr. Crow said, "Let's walk to the end of the row here."

It was there that our pastor asked, "Mr. Arthur, I've just come to introduce myself and share Jesus with you."

"I'm ready for Jesus. You just need to tell me what I need to do."

There between the rows of peas Arthur Crow, in simple faith, turned his life and heart over to Jesus. He asked for forgiveness of his sins and "a new start."

And that's just what he got. He was a new man. It was evident to everyone in Dry Creek. He had a quiet joy in the Lord and became a faithful member of our church.

When Mr. Arthur was buried this week, Don Hunt couldn't be there. He's battling cancer and has been extremely ill.

I called Bro. Don this morning and listened as he joyfully recalled what I'm now sharing with you. I reminded him, "Arthur Crow is in heaven because of your witness."

His reply was, "I just arrived at the right time. He was ready due to a lifetime of praying by his family and church."

I know he's right on that, but Don Hunt had the courage and love to step across the field to share with his neighbor. And on that day, a man was ready for new life and new birth.

Sometimes I wonder if it's easier to fly to Africa to share about Jesus than to walk across the pea patch to a neighbor. It shouldn't be, but it can seem harder.

However, it's no excuse for me not to.

Jesus talks about it in Acts 1:8: Jerusalem, Judea (our area), Samaria (anywhere where it's difficult), and the ends of the Earth.

It's not a multiple-choice quiz. He calls us to be involved in some form in each area.

It may be the Bush area of Liberia or a Piney Woods pea patch.

Either way, it's a privilege.

It's also a responsibility.

A Pair for Life

Clay, Clint, and I crawled over the wet leaves to the bluff bank on the small stream called Dry Creek. We were just west of where it runs into Bundick's Creek. Crawling along, I kept looking at the boys reminding them to stay quiet. Silence was needed because I knew I had heard wood ducks on the water.

Sliding along to the cliff edge, we saw them—a male drake resplendent in the beautiful colors that make the wood duck my favorite bird. He was swimming along beside his drab colored hen companion. They nervously swam in circles, fully aware of something being wrong, but couldn't quite place where we were.

It was a special moment in my life—one of my sons on each side lying on the high bank—as we watched the pair of ducks swimming about.

The boys kept glancing back—at my shotgun, which was leaning against a nearby tree. I shook my head as they imploringly looked at me. We lay there about ten minutes watching them. Eventually the ducks swam down Dry Creek, out into the stronger current of Bundick's Creek . . . and then were gone.

My sons upbraided me about not shooting the ducks. I tried explaining how they were a pair. If my understanding of waterfowl was correct, they were a couple just the same as their mom and me. I just didn't have the heart to shoot. I'm not sure the boys understood, but one day they probably will.

I thought about that pair of ducks when we buried my grandmother. As I sat with my grandfather at the hospital before her death and then at the funeral, my mind kept returning to those two ducks in the creek—a pair for life.

Grandpa and Grandma Sid, as we called them, were married over sixty-two years when she died. Throughout my memory, they only existed together—inseparable. Whenever, and wherever I saw them, they were together—my Grandpa and Grandma Sid.

Sitting beside him at the funeral, I thought about how they were no longer together. How it hurt my heart seeing him alone. How lonely it must have been after spending practically every moment together over the last twenty years and sharing life together for over sixty.

I thought about my own wife, DeDe, and how close we are. And I thought about the loneliness one of us will one day endure.

Once again, I could see the wood ducks swimming off together.

It occurred to me how long sixty-two years must be—and how quickly sixty-two years must seem to pass. My grandfather's words came back, "Well, if I'd had her ninety-two years, I still wouldn't have wanted to give her up."

There are so many things I don't understand about life. It is full of so much happiness and sadness. We live and love the same person for a lifetime of happiness, and then it must end sadly—and alone.

We must choose. We can concentrate on the happy memories and joy shared together—this intertwining of two lives wrapped together by love, or we can dwell on the sorrow and loneliness that comes to us when "death does us part."

I choose thinking about those two happy wood ducks swimming off into the current together paired with a heart full of wonderful memories of my grandparents.

Leaning Trees

"When I observe a young person I experience two strong emotions. First, I feel great affection for the young person they are. Then secondly, I feel a deep respect for the adult they will one day become."

-Louis Pasteur

On the morning before Hurricane Rita arrived, I made one last survey of my tree farm. Sadly, I knew it would never look the same.

In our part of Louisiana, there are thousands of acres of pine tree plantations, or tree farms. Grown in rows for future harvesting, they are the backbone of our economy. Most tree farms are large and owned by forestry companies. Others, like mine, are small and owned by private landowners.

I'd pampered my fifteen acres of slash pines since their planting seven years prior. I'd bushogged among them, killed the invading tallow trees, and faithfully plowed around the perimeter yearly protecting them from fire.

My fear had always been damage from a storm. Slash pines grow fast and make good trees but have a weakness at a young age if they encounter an ice storm or hurricane. They were at the most vulnerable age, and I worried that many would not survive.

The storm arrived during the night. At our Church Camp we were so busy with three hundred evacuees that I didn't have time to worry about my trees. Our guests were a blend of Katrina evacuees and coastal residents who had fled this new storm. This night together was long, memorable, and one I hope never to repeat.

Daylight on Saturday revealed unbelievable damage on the campgrounds. Trees were broken and splintered and electrical lines were down everywhere. Finally, the wind subsided and it was safe enough to drive home.

A lump was in my throat as I approached our house. The smallest pines were in the front section of my tree farm. These three-year-old trees were about six-feet high. Many are bent over, leaning toward the northwest giving testimony about the ferocity of the hurricane that battered Dry Creek during the night.

Happily, the larger rows of trees in the back field have come through the storm well. Some are leaning and others are broken off wherever there was a weak spot, but overall they are fine. However, my smaller trees look beyond help and I begin mentally planning on cutting them and starting over on this section.

༄

Two weeks after the hurricane, State Forester Paul Frey spoke in DeRidder. His words, quoted in the Beauregard Daily News, caught my attention:

"I urge you timber owners not to give up on trees that may be leaning but are still firmly rooted. Don't give up on them. From previous history and previous experience, they will eventually straighten back out. Don't give up on eighteen years of growth and lose the investment you've made."

His words echo in my heart. "Eighteen years … of growth … don't give up … and lose that investment … they will straighten up if that root system is firm and rooted."

Suddenly, I'm not thinking about pine trees and hurricanes. I'm thinking about teenagers. I've worked with young people all of my adult life, first as a teacher and coach, later as a school principal, and then as administrator of a church youth camp.

I've seen my share of leaning teens, I mean trees . . .

no, I really do mean leaning teens. The teenage years are difficult years for a young person as well as those around them, especially parents. Many times, just like my wind-ravaged pines, they lean badly and seem damaged beyond recovery.

But teens, like trees, are resilient, especially if their root system is firm, deep, and strong. Don't give up on them. There's a lot of future growth and good return ahead.

Here's a word for any discouraged parents: Don't give up on a leaning teenager. Just help ensure their root system is strong and firm.

Look down the road to the future—don't count them off as a loss and lose your "future investment." I've seen it many times—leaning teens later becoming strong and secure adults.

ꟷ

Thinking of leaning teens, Vance comes to mind. Now, Vance was never a bad teenager, but he did lean some during his high school years. I was his basketball coach and he will always be one of my favorite players. His play on the court was signified by passion, a slashing style of play that was sometimes reckless, but always joyful to watch.

That passion was reflected in his personal life. In addition to his athleticism, Vance was, and is, a master musician. He has a rich baritone country voice and guitar playing style that touches anyone who hears him.

In his years after high school, his music led him to play in the honky-tonks and bars, where his style and songs made him popular. Vance would be the first in admitting he did some leaning away from the Lord during these years. Then, just like my young pines, he began a straightening process. Not an overnight change, but a gradual, steady, and lasting course correction from the Lord. A process of becoming the man he is now.

The only leaning Vance does now is leaning over during church and saying to the other musicians, "The key of G on the next song." Every Sunday he is on stage using his marvelous gift for God's glory.

Sitting at my drums listening to the heavenly guitar playing coming from Vance's fingers, I'm hearing living proof of the importance of not giving up on leaning teenagers.

In the weeks after the hurricane, I studied my bent pines. Amazingly, most of them slowly but steadily began straightening up. Time, patience, and the wonderful combination of nature, sunlight, rain, and nutrition made the difference as they once again reached for the sky.

A few pines are broken and will need cutting. Others will always have a lean, but that's O.K. They will serve as "testimony trees." Driving by my tree farm, fathers will say to their children, "When I was a boy, Hurricane Rita came through here. That tall slash pine there is now about forty-years-old. It was small when the storm hit and still has a slight lean—Rita did that. Yep, that was one bad storm."

Lessons from my tree farm.
The many lessons from a storm,
from a destructive hurricane named Rita:
The strong firm foundational lesson
of not giving up on leaning trees.

ꕥ

Train up a child in the way he should go,
and when he is old, he will not depart from it.
-Proverbs 22:6 KJV

Trespassing

I don't consider myself a poet, but recorded this as a iPhone voice memo during a recent hike of the Wild Azalea Trail, a thirty-mile hiking path extending through central Louisiana's Kisatchie National Forest.

He sees me about the same time I see him.
And I'm trespassing.
Trespassing on his land.
He knows it, and so do I.

All that's behind me is a bridge and creek
I can't go back.
So I watch him carefully.
As I step around him and his web.

The biggest garden spider I've ever seen.
With a web worthy of his size,
stretching across the trail.
I could destroy his web, and charge on through.

But I've learned to be respectful on someone else's land.
So with a tip of my hat, I ease around.
The sun reflects off his yellow and black abdomen.
I wish him well and hurry down the winding trail.

Measure Twice, Cut Once

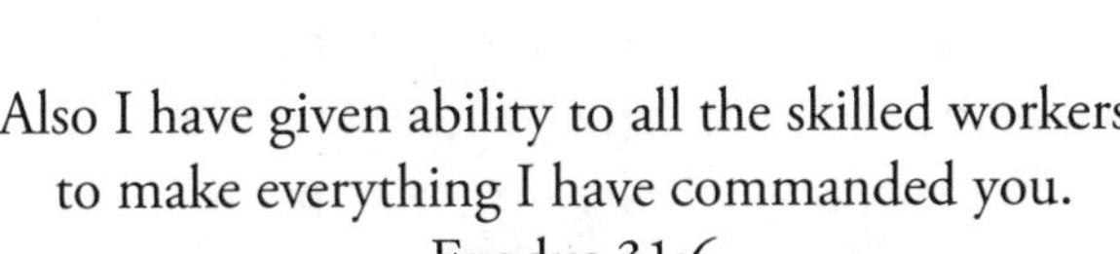

Also I have given ability to all the skilled workers
to make everything I have commanded you.
-Exodus 31:6

I've always loved watching an artist at work. To watch a skilled craftsman shape something with their hands—and heart—is a joy.

As the above verse in Exodus states, the work of a gifted craftsman is a gift from God. The fact that great artists have honed their skills with hundreds of hours of repetitious practice makes it no less a gift from God. In fact, it must please God greatly to see someone take a gifted skill and be a good steward in developing it.

Author Malcolm Gladwell, in his excellent book *Outliers*, sums this up, "It takes about 10,000 hours to become really great at anything."

In my hometown of Dry Creek, two artisans are my close friends. They both operate under the wise motto of "measure twice, cut once." It just happens that they're married to each other.

Van is a carpenter. He is a tall sinewy man with a quick smile and strong hands.

He works hard and is known for doing good and dependable work. As a carpenter, he knows all about "measuring twice before cutting once."

Waste is not a quality for a good carpenter. Carefully measuring to get it right the first time eliminates a lot of grief later on. You may not think of a carpenter as an artist, but they are. Webster's defines an artist as "one who is adept at something."

The second artist is Van's wife, Cathy. She operates In Style Hair Salon in Dry Creek. On my monthly trip to get my bald-head clipped, I'm amazed as I watch her hands move quickly cutting, styling, and shaping the hair of the men and women of our community.

Cathy also operates by the "measure twice—cut once" principle. She told of a customer who made five trips in one day—each time wanting a "little bit more cut off."

Knowing that "once it's cut, it's gone," Cathy carefully trimmed a little bit more, knowing the customer was near the "I can't believe I got that much cut off" line.

Measure twice, cut once.

It's a good motto for anyone, not just a hair stylist or a carpenter.

Cathy was the first woman to cut my dad's hair at the age of sixty-three. He told me, "I did something today I'd never done. I had a woman cut my hair."

A few years ago after his death, Cathy said, "I still have a lock of your daddy's hair. When he became sick with cancer, I kept a lock in honor and memory of him.

That meant the world to me.

80

I've had unforgettable haircuts in two foreign countries—Vietnam and Ethiopia.

During my 2002 visit to Vietnam, I was amused at the barbershops in the capital city of Hanoi. In the parks, barbers would hang a mirror on a tree, pull up a chair, and cut hair with scissors and a straight razor.

I decided to get one these outdoor haircuts. The only problem was that my barber didn't speak English and I didn't know Vietnamese. I figured sign language would work just fine. Holding my thumb and forefinger a half-inch apart, I gestured, "Just a little. Not much."

The barber smiled, popped his apron, and put me in the chair. He quickly went to work. Because we couldn't talk, there was none of the "story breaks" I was used to in America.

The Viet barber had me turned away from his mirror. Even without looking, I knew he was cutting off too much. The amount of hair falling onto the apron and ground alarmed me.

When he pulled out the straight razor, I'd had enough. He looked to be about my age and had probably fought with the Viet Cong or North Vietnamese Army. There was no way he was going to put a razor on my neck.

Standing up, I looked into the mirror and saw that I'd been scalped.

I realized that my two-fingered gesture of "cut just a little" was interpreted as "leave just a little."

I don't recall how many Viet đồng my haircut cost, but I definitely got my money's worth. When my American friends saw me, one said, "What in the world happened to you?"

"Oh, I just got a Hanoi haircut."

Fortunately, there was a week before we left for home. By the time we re-crossed the Pacific and returned to America, my hair had mostly recovered from my Hanoi haircut.

You'd think I would have learned from my Vietnam experience, but in Ethiopia, I bravely entered a barbershop as DeDe asked, "Are you sure you want to do this?"

The shop was full of men laughing and talking until the Furanji (their derisive term for foreigners) entered. The young barber motioned me into his chair. His trembling hands were ample proof that he'd never cut a white man's hair.

He took a deep breath, then poured alcohol on his clippers, struck a match, and placed it in front of my face. I probably should have run right then.

He was only showing me that he'd sterilized his clippers. Those clippers buzzed loudly around my ears as he went to work. I noticed that everyone in the shop stopped talking and the other barbers quit cutting. They were intent on watching my haircut. I felt sorry for the barber. He was under the gun.

As I watched the mirror, I would smile and approvingly shake my head in encouragement.

He finished and the entire room, including DeDe, seemed to exhale together. I paid my money, left him a good tip, and waved goodbye to the audience who'd watched my Ethiopian haircut.

The young barber walked us to the door, shaking my hand and talking in Amharic. I'll always wonder what he was saying.

As I put my ball cap on and we strolled away, he looked up and down the street as if looking for the next furanji who might invade his barbershop.

I wonder how you translate "Measure Twice-Cut Once" into Ethiopian Amharic?

The Friendship Lane

The most important trip you may take in life is meeting people halfway.
–Henry Boye

Here's a question: for what price would you sell your friendship? What amount of money would entice you to turn your back on a neighbor, friend, or family member?

Most of us easily answer, "No amount of money."

That's the correct answer but I often wonder if it's what our actions say. I've seen folks fall out over a family heirloom or perceived slight. I watched a brother and sister fall out over a three-foot-wide strip of inherited land.

This story is about two men who refused to lose their friendship over a difference of opinion. It is a story worth telling.

It's a story worth remembering.

To tell you the story of "The Friendship Lane," I must take you there. So let's walk together to an overgrown path in the woods. Most people will walk right by this narrow passageway and never notice it, but it always catches my attention because of what it means.

It is located just east of Dry Creek Camp's property line. It is a ten-foot wide strip between two barbed wire fences. This path separates the land between the pioneer homesteads of Sereno Hanchey and Lionel Green. These two men, now dead for many years, were descendants of some of the earliest settlers of Dry Creek.

Mr. Rufus Hanchey, Sereno Hanchey's son, took me to

"The Friendship Lane" just before he died. As we stood there, he related the following story:

"Curt, at some point many years ago, there was a difference of opinion between the Hanchey and Green families over where the property line was. Each family claimed ownership on land that reached over into the other's present field. Because no fence marked the dividing line, the actual land line was open to dispute."

Mr. Rufus continued, "My dad and Lionel Green had always been good friends, and they valued their friendship more than any piece of land—and showed it by their subsequent actions. They met at the very spot we are now standing and came up with a solution for this problem. They declared the disputed ten-foot wide strip a 'neutral zone.' Each man would build a fence on his respective side of the strip. Together, they agreed on using the strip as a pathway on which neither family would claim ownership. Due to this arrangement, both families were satisfied and no further problem ever occurred."

As the son of a land surveyor, I've seen some nasty fights between landowners over the difference of a two-foot strip along a fence. Some of the saddest things I've ever seen have been family members falling out over land, often going to their graves still holding a grudge. How sad it is when we will let anything, material or temporary, break a priceless relationship with our families or neighbors.

Now, I'm proud of the little plot of land I own. There is something special about walking your field and knowing the mud on your boots is yours. However, when I feel as if this land really belongs to me, I get out my land abstract.

An abstract is a legal booklet showing the history of ownership of the land you own. Thumbing through my abstract, I recognize some of the old family names that once lived in this area. It strikes me that some of these once well-known family surnames are no longer found in our area. They are now only names from the distant past.

A sobering thought materializes: One day the land I live on will belong to someone else. They'll look at their updated abstract and wonder who the Iles family was that once lived here.

My visit with Mr. Rufus reminded me that my own land really doesn't belong to me. He had wisely stated that day during our visit to the woods, "Son, we don't own this land; it owns us. It really belongs to God. He's just loaning it to us for this short finite period of time we call life."

Standing reverently with Mr. Rufus in the middle of The Friendship Lane, I was appreciative of his story of these two men who'd placed friendship above an easily forgotten strip of land. People, and the relationships we develop through friendship, are much more important than any land title we can store in a safety deposit box.

The Friendship Lane teaches another lesson—if we're going to get along with others, we must give them a little room. Young people today call it "cutting some slack." If we push against, and rub on others, friction will result. And friction always generates heat, and heat can generate the fire of anger that, in time, can harm and ruin longtime friendships.

By simply giving others some space and walking away instead of fighting, the "friendship fences" in our lives can stay mended and in good shape. If we always must "win" by getting our way, we will leave behind a trail of broken relationships, many of them with those closest to us. I am often reminded of the saying, "You only have so much blood to spill, so choose your battles carefully."

Darkness is now approaching as I turn and leave Mr. Rufus and the Friendship Lane. Glancing back one last time, I visualize in my mind the long ago scene of Sereno Hanchey and Lionel Green walking their respective fields at sunset. They come upon each other and stop for a visit. Each leans against his own fence, separated by the ten feet of land they share.

First one, then the other, crawls through his fence. They

meet in this grassy neutral area where they shake hands, share a plug of chewing tobacco, and visit until it is so dark you can barely see them.

Only from the sound of their laughter and low voices, can you tell they are standing back there somewhere.

Meeting man to man in the middle of the Friendship Lane.

The richest man in the world is not the one who still has the first dollar he has ever earned. It is the man who still has his best friends.

You're the Man

I'd never heard of the Broken Wings Award until recently.

I haven't met helicopter pilot Edwin Steve Coleman, one of the few two-time winners of the award.

I believe I'd like Chief Warrant Officer Coleman.

Before you meet him, you need to understand what the Broken Wings Award is about. To win it, a pilot must safely bring a crippled aircraft down. The problem cannot be pilot-caused and the pilot must get the machine down with minimal damage to property and life.

Coleman first won the award eighteen years ago in Czechoslovakia, but that's another story for another day. This is the story of how he won his second Broken Wings in 2006 over the skies—and among the piney woods—of Louisiana.

Coleman and a co-pilot were flying an OH-58 Charlie helicopter over a heavily forested area of Ft. Polk. Suddenly the copter's engine died, forcing Coleman to make several quick decisions.

Helicopter engine failure normally leads to horrific crashes, usually accompanied by fatalities. Landing a "dead copter" is a quick and grim fight with death.

From an article in the January 2007 "Beauregard Daily News," Officer Coleman recalled that day. "When something goes wrong, you must keep the rotors moving in order to have any control. Due to our low height of 400 feet and our speed of 40 knots, there was no time or room for error."

This is when his training kicked in. He stood on the brakes to make the aircraft stand vertical on its tail. As gravity took over, he was able to negotiate the controls and maneuver the copter toward a small clearing.

Before impact he told his co-pilot, "This is going to hurt."

Neither pilot was injured in the rough landing, and the helicopter suffered little damage. As the dust cleared and the rotors stopped turning, the two men stared in relief and amazement at the small clearing surrounded by tall pines. The younger co-pilot reached across the cockpit, shook Officer Coleman's hand, and solemnly said, "You're the man!"

You're the man. That says it all.

It's the term we want those around us to say.

Most of all, we want our family saying it honestly about us.

You are the man. You are respected. Esteemed.

John Avant, pastor of West Monroe's First Baptist Church, uses this life motto, "To be a man that God can use, and be respected by my wife and children."

That says it all—you are the man. If God can use you, and your family holds you in respect, you are the man.

What others think—and say—pales in comparison if your Creator and family are pleased.

Conversely, for a man to be esteemed at work or in the world, but not by those closest to him—is not really a success.

More importantly, being used by God and seeking to please Him is the greatest success of all. It has nothing to do with being chauvinistic or domineering. Rather, it's about servant-leadership. The towel-toting, foot-washing, life-sacrificing kind that Jesus lived.

Yes, Chief Warrant Officer Edwin Steve Coleman was "the man" in the skies above the Louisiana piney woods. He was a pilot who knew what to do.

೩೦

They've just started road construction on the highway we live on. The paving company has a vehicle with a large sign atop it reading "Pilot Car—Follow Me."

To control the traffic flow through the construction zone,

cars must follow this lead vehicle. As I put my truck in gear, I obediently followed in the pilot car's exact tracks as it dodged potholes and meandered around equipment.

Pilot Car—Follow Me.

The inference is "I know what I'm doing and where I'm going, so follow me."

Similar to being in the cockpit with Captain Coleman.

The pilot car reminded me of what I am as a man. Others—my family, younger people, and those in my community—are studying my life. Whether I want to wear the sign or not, my life says, "Pilot Car—Follow Me."

That's a scary thought. Whether I lead right or wrong, someone is following me. Therefore, I had better lead in the right way.

That pilot car on Highway 394 leads a trail of vehicles past my house. I bet if it veered off the road shoulder at Mill Bayou and plunged into the creek, someone would follow dutifully, and as their car bogged down to the frame, holler out the window, "It said, 'Pilot Car—Follow Me."

As a man, I'm driving the pilot car, whether I want to be or not.

I hope to drive and lead in a way that those behind me will say, "You're the man."

I'll end this flight with a short prayer. A prayer from the heart of the man writing this.

"Jesus, you're the real Man. If you don't lead me, I can't lead anyone. Teach me to lead. Lead through me. Amen."

Bro. Hodges' Best Sermon

The preacher stood in the middle of the muddy red clay road staring at the problem straight ahead. He was about three miles from his pulpit, and was going to preach "his best sermon" in a few minutes.

This white-suited minister straddling a mud hole was Kenneth Hodges, my pastor as a teenager. He was a tall and lanky man—skinny with a large Adam's apple, long nose, and unruly black hair. To me he looked like a character from a Norman Rockewll painting. It wasn't his physical appearance that made him special—it was his loving spirit and kindness toward everyone.

He was also the most down-to-earth pastor I've ever known—and that is why everyone in Dry Creek loved him. He was a "what you see is what you get" kind of guy, and where I come from, that's a high compliment.

"WYSIWYG." What you see is what you get. No pretense. No artificial flavoring. Down to earth.

Kenneth Hodges became our pastor in the early 1970s and soon after that became "the pastor" to everyone in the community—whether they were churchgoers or not. He had a great ability to connect with all types of people.

Bro. Hodges could preach a good sermon; but what he did best was "pastor." He cared about people and it showed daily in dozens of kind acts. I've always believed the following story of kindness was his "best sermon":

On the Monday of this story, Bro. Hodges dressed up in his best suit. I can still see it—a white leisure suit with blue stitching and buttons with white patent-leather shoes. I always told him he looked like the Easter Bunny. He was going "into town" to a meeting, but first planned on dropping by to check on an elderly congregation member, who lived off the highway on Joe Gray Road.

Country people can understand what I'm saying here—there is nothing worse than a red clay road after a rain in the winter months. Joe Gray Road was that type of road. It was a full time job just keeping his old Buick between the ditches. Navigating around a slick curve, Bro. Hodges came upon a problem in the road.

One of the local farmers stood in the road trying to round up three horses. The horses were definitely winning. If you've ever tried to re-fence animals, you can picture the futility and frustration of this farmer.

Bro. Hodges stopped his vehicle. I'm sure he looked at the horses, muddy road, and his white suit. The easy thing would've been to drive on by with a word of encouragement to the farmer.

Except he didn't do the easy thing. That was not his style. He got out, joined the rodeo, and helped get the horses back behind the fence. Needless to say, after the horses were corralled, the suit wasn't white. In fact, it and the shoes were caked with red mud and ruined—never to be worn again.

Bro. Hodges didn't tell this story to anyone—he didn't have to. The farmer, not a church-going man, told it at the post office-clearing house that serves as the dispenser of information in rural communities.

In a few short days, everyone knew the story of the wrangler-preacher and his rodeo on Joe Gray Road. It's true that bad news travels fast, but sometimes good news can travel even faster.

I'll always believe this was his finest sermon ever. It was one preached in love and with willing hands and feet—a sermon that lives on in my heart and mind. It's the type of story that bears repeating. So pass it on.

Kenneth Hodges was my pastor during the most formative

years of my life. I cannot honestly remember one specific sermon he preached from the pulpit, but his sermon on the muddy road lives on—as it should.

Postscript

A few years after the above story occurred, Bro. Hodges died in an accident in Dry Creek. His death occurred as he was doing what he did best—helping others. He is still remembered and loved by those of us who knew him.

"Greater love hath no man than this
that a man lay down his life for his friends."
-John 15:13

Whippoorwill Day

"There is no quiet place in the white man's cities. No place to hear the leaves of spring, or the rustle of insect wings. What is there to life if a man cannot hear the lovely cry of the whippoorwill or the arguments of the frogs around the pond at night?"

-Chief Seattle
Meeting with President Franklin Pierce
Washington, D.C. 1855

It's a day I always look forward to—the 6th day of April.

It's "Whippoorwill Day."

My great grandmother, who was born after the Civil War and lived for over half of the next century, always said, "If you go down in the edge of the swamp on the sixth day of April, you'll hear a whippoorwill calling. You can set your clock by it."

I'm writing this a few weeks after the date—in the gathering darkness of a late April evening—and a whippoorwill is serenading non-stop. I'm sitting beside a lake in rural Evangeline Parish where this bird has been calling for thirty minutes without taking a breath.

Before I tell you more about Whippoorwill Day, you must know about the bird itself. A member of the nightjar family, these groups of long-winged birds, sometimes referred to as "goatsuckers," are mainly nocturnal. During the day, whippoorwills roost quietly in trees and are rarely spotted due to their natural camouflage. In a lifetime of woods roaming, I've only seen one, and it was dead on the road, evidently the casualty of a vehicle collision.

Whippoorwills are migratory birds passing through Louisiana twice a year. As they stop on their southward fall migration, they are silent. Then, as cooler weather approaches, they are driven southward, spending the winter months in Central and South America.

With the advent of spring, the whippoorwills return north and stop in Louisiana. On this trip, they bring their voices. Sometimes they are heard in late March, but normally it's April before the evenings and mornings are filled with their calling. The old-timers knew the bird's song as a true harbinger of warm weather. Many would not plant their southern peas until they heard the bird singing, giving rise to the term, "whippoorwill peas."

On their spring sojourn, they make up for the shy silence of fall. During the courtship season, they'll often call all night. I've camped out and listened to a lover's triangle through the entire night. If you ever hear one, you'll know exactly what it is. Its call is its name—"whip-poor-will" with the accent on the first and last syllables. Its lonely call has been part of the woodland lore. Stories, songs, and tales have sprung up from this secretive bird.

Great-Grandma Doten's April 6 day was primary among these tales.

I'll always tenderly recall my grandfather's last year on earth. After the death of my grandmother, he moved in with my parents. When April 6 arrived, he and I ventured into the swamp and leaned on a fence, listening to the silence of the woods.

We waited. No whippoorwills.

The mosquitoes began biting, and I was concerned about my grandpa falling in the darkness, so we turned toward the house. Just then, a faraway whippoorwill began calling. In the dark, I couldn't see Grandpa's face, but the joy in his words was clear. "That bird's song makes it worth it all."

As we made our way carefully out of the swamp, he reminisced about a lifetime of studying and loving birds. Every step of ours echoed against the bird's rhythmic calling. It was an experience that still moves me as I relive it.

It was his last Whippoorwill Day, and it will always be my favorite one.

Rural people had many beliefs and superstitions about this bird: if you were the first to hear one answer back on April 6, your future spouse would be thinking about you that day. Other beliefs were more troubling: a person on their deathbed couldn't die until a whippoorwill called three times.

℘

Back at my lakeside listening station, the whippoorwill serenading me has switched positions. His calls become more spaced apart and softer. It's about time for him to clock in on the evening shift of snagging insects from the night sky.

A nearby train drowns out his song as I return inside.

Sadly, this past April 6 featured no whippoorwill songs in my swamp. My family has lived on this land for over one hundred and twenty years and nearly every April 6 has been blessed with the singing of the spring visitor.

The last ten years have been sporadic at best. I've read that the American whippoorwill population is in steady decline. I knew that without reading it. Every April has fewer mornings and evenings filled with its memorable repetitive calls.

It wouldn't matter if I never heard another call on April 6. It will always be "Whippoorwill Day" to me because some things are not just heard with the ears, but also deep in the heart.

And things of the heart never disappear.

"Did you ever hear a whippoorwill
Who sounds too blue to fly.
It seems he's lost the one he loves,
I'm so lonesome I could cry."
_-Hank Williams, Sr.
"I'm So Lonesome I Could Cry."

The Miller Oak

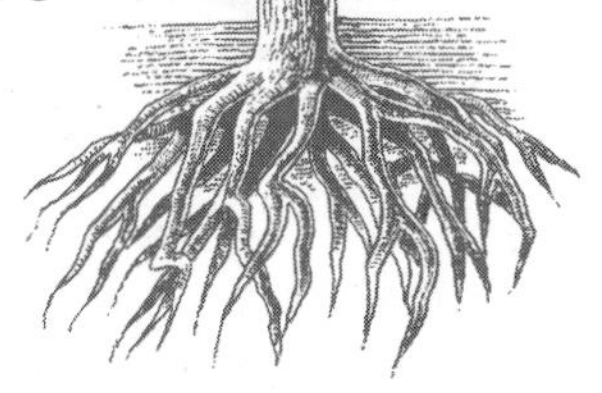

There's a majestic cherry bark oak that sits at the entrance of Dry Creek Baptist Camp.

It's not just another tree. It's the Miller Oak and there's a wonderful story behind its name.

Cherry bark oaks are one of the dozen species of red oak family. They produce the highest quality lumber of any red oaks and are highly valued by sawmills. According to my resident forester, my son Clint, cherry bark oaks grade higher because of their strength, absence of knots, resistant to rot, and "clear wood."

Firewood cutters love the red oaks because of their ease in splitting due to the rich red heart in the center of the trunk. When Hurricane Rita blew through our community, we showed our sense of humor on a banner:

Dry Creek Forecast:
Plenty of firewood this winter!

As the storm approached, I wondered if this old giant called the Miller Oak could withstand the storm. It always looked healthy but you never know. One of the amazing discoveries after a hurricane is to see fallen trees that seemed firm and healthy but had a hollow or rotten spot inside.

It often takes a storm to reveal an interior flaw. That kind of reminds me about life. There are plenty of storms in our lives … many external like a hurricane, while others are internal … but regardless, a storm will reveal the true character of the person. If there is weakness, no matter how well hidden, the storm will reveal the truth.

As Joe Moore told his son, Mayo, in the novel, A *Good*

Place. "Son, a storm doesn't build character in a man. It simply reveals it."

I'm thankful that I'm not depending on my inner strength because I've got plenty of knots and hollow spots. But the Jesus inside me—"Greater is He that is in you"—is plenty strong enough to take whatever blows my way.

The morning after Hurricane Rita, I ran outside in the gray misty light of dawn to check on the Miller Oak. Only one small limb had dropped from it. This Dry Creek cherry bark oak had withstood the storm.

Forester Clint's words come back: "highest grade, least knots, clearest wood, worth three times as much as other red oak lumber."

What a symbol for strength in the storm. I stepped back from the oak and saluted it in love and respect.

I'm not sure how old this oak tree is but it was big enough for a teenage girl named Lois McFatter to remember it. Here, from her memoir is the story of "The Big Oak":

"It was August of 1928. I recognized Frank Miller of Dry Creek coming through the main gate of the encampment. With him was his brother Ray, whom he brought over for me to meet. Ray was tall … very handsome, and the vibes between us were electric and we began dating."

You can probably guess the rest of this story. This Dry Creek boy and Ragley girl married and lived a long life of serving God together in Calcasieu Parish. Just recently, Mrs. Lois McFatter Miller died at age 91 and rejoined in Heaven that "tall handsome boy" she met under the Big Oak at Dry Creek.

So this Big Oak has a name: it's the Miller Oak. It symbolizes to me something that still happens during summer camp at Dry Creek. A boy meets a girl. A girl notices a boy. They fall in love.

In a lifetime at camp I've heard literally hundreds of stories of romances that began at camp. I've seen dozens bloom myself.

Each summer as our teenage and college staff arrived in May we'd seat them in a circle. The thirty of them sat giggling nervously. They were beginning a journey after which they would never be the same. Regardless of whether they know each other now, many will become lifelong friends after a summer together.

I knew that some in this circle would fall in love … and it might last for a lifetime.

Just like the marriage of Ray and Lois Miller … "To death do us part …" Solid just like that old majestic cherry bark oak greeting visitors to the camp for nearly ninety years.

But still standing tall,

Not ready yet to surrender to Rita's winds or Bro. Eugene's chain saw.

It's my favorite tree in downtown Dry Creek … It's a cherry bark oak.

I call it the Miller Oak.

A Prophet has no Honor

This true story is nearly too good to be true. As a fiction writer and historian, I've learned that you cannot make up a story that's better than the truth.

My next-door neighbors are Mark and Mitzi Foreman. The Foremans, and their two children, Mavy and Mark Jr., operate Foreman's Meat Market at the intersection of Highways 113 and 394.

This story is not meant as a commercial, but if you've never eaten boudin or sausage from Foreman's, you haven't lived. They are known far and wide for their wonderful Cajun-seasoned meats. Our son, Clint, loves to get his mom's shopping list and add, "Buy plenty of Foreman's sausage."

At Foreman's, you can buy stuffed chicken breasts and pork chops, along with a greasy paper bag of fresh fried cracklings, which are authentic crunchy pork skins. Northerners may make fun of the South but they know our food can't be beat.

At the 2007 National Championship game between L.S.U. and The Ohio State University, a Louisiana fan waved a sign: "Better food, hotter women, and faster players."

I agree on all three points.

Mark and Mitzi Foreman opened their Dry Creek store in 1993. They've been very successful due to a great location, a quality product, and lots of hard work.

This story is not about them. It's about their son, Mark, known in our community as "Boom-Boom." For the sake of simplicity, I'll call him Mark, but if you come in Foreman's Grocery, ask for Boom-Boom.

Mark Jr. is a businessman and sausage expert just like

his dad. Presently, his responsibility is making cracklings at the store. He can also discuss, in detail, the fine points of red pepper, casings, and correct sausage cooking times. My boys sat with him on the school bus, and they related how he constantly sketched sausage-making equipment and smokehouses. I predict Mark will one day be rich and famous as an entrepreneur, far beyond the confines of Dry Creek.

This specific story happened when Mark was about ten years old. At this age, he began attending Catechism, which is where Catholic doctrine is taught. The very first lesson, from the Old Testament, told about the early patriarchs of the Bible. As the teacher introduced the stories of Moses, Abraham, and Isaiah, she asked this question, "Do any of you know what a prophet is?"

The children looked at each other waiting to see who'd answer first. However, they shouldn't have waited, because Mark Foreman already knew the answer and excitedly waved his hand back and forth.

The teacher asked, "Mark, do you know what a *prophet* is?"

Without any hesitation, he answered, "A prophet is the money you have left over in your business, after you've paid all of your bills."

Fully satisfied with his excellent answer, this future business tycoon sat down. I'm not sure if he passed Introduction to the Old Testament, but I'll bet you a bag of hot cracklings he'll pass Economics 101.

30 Years Ago

As the older woman wrote the check, her billfold lay open on the counter. I saw the picture—a graduation photo carefully placed in the front.

The photo featured a handsome smiling young man with blonde hair.

I hesitated to mention it but knew I must. “That’s your son Mark.”

She stopped and smiled. “I’m always so happy when someone remembers him.”

I said, “I remember Mark well and loved watching him on the basketball court.” Tears joined her smile, as I continued, “His Elizabeth High team was a hard-working and cohesive one, and I’ll always remember the part Mark played on it.”

We shared tenderly of memories of her long dead son. It had been about thirty years since Mark’s death in a car accident while coming home from college.

Three decades later, his mother still had his photo right where it should be—in the front of her billfold. I was humbled and amazed as I intimately observed that divine thing called a mother’s love.

She handed her check, and I placed an autographed book in her hand. As she walked away, I knew we had exchanged more than two paper objects—we had exchanged hearts.

I’d let her know Mark was not forgotten. In return she had given me a glimpse into her heart—a mother’s heart. A heart still full of tender grief, yet also full of sweet love.

It's approaching Mother's Day, and I've thought often of Mark's photo. As I see it in my heart, I also recall the love, light, and lingering sorrow on his mother's face. It was a look that only a mother can project.

I've also pondered another mother. A mother who understood all about love, grief, and loss. Her name was Mary, and as the years pass my admiration, respect, and love grows for this woman chosen by God to raise His one and only Son.

That's a tall order: rearing the Savior of the World.

It's a high calling. One that I don't think God took lightly when He chose Mary and Joseph. I know it's a responsibility she took seriously.

In these thoughts of the mother of Jesus, I always see her at the foot of the cross. Others may have run, but mothers don't. They are always there for you. I know firsthand—I have that kind of mother.

I can only imagine the pain as Mary watched her amazing Son suffer. How much did she understand about His calling and mission? I'm not sure, but no amount of insight could have prepared her for watching her son die.

I'm further amazed when I hear her son speak from the cross. He nods toward his best friend, John. "Son, that's your mother."

Then he reassures her with a gesture of his head. "Mother, that's your son."

There is no way His words and dying gestures can be misunderstood. John and Mary are now linked for life.

Mary is a personal observer of her Son's resurrection three days later, but don't think her grief in watching Him suffer and die was lessened.

Nor should the fact that he didn't die again, but ascended directly into heaven, make us underestimate her pain. Mary still missed him. Her Son was gone, and she couldn't touch Him or talk with Him.

The Biblical record is silent on how long Mary lived after Jesus left this earth.

But I wonder if it might have been thirty years.

Or even more. Maybe, like Mark's mother, she lived more years after he was gone than he had been alive. It happens.

And I wonder how Mary missed Him. She didn't carry a photograph in her billfold, but carried one in her heart.

The love of a mother.

It transcends the years.

It lives on in spite of death and loss.

I firmly believe it is probably the closest thing on this earth to the divine love of God.

A mother's love. A love of the heart.

The Ripple Effect

*"Do all the good you can, in all the ways you can,
In all the places you can,
At all the times you can,
To all the people you can,
As long as ever you can."
-John Wesley*

The numbers tell the story better than I ever could. 1, then 2, 62, and finally 42,679. Those are the numbers of the ripple effect.

The date was the summer of 2004, and the place was Minute Maid Park in Houston, Texas.

There's nothing I like better than watching my beloved Houston Astros play baseball at home. What makes this experience even better is taking a large group of young people, many of whom have never set foot inside a major league stadium.

There are sixty-two of us sitting in the left field nosebleed seats. It is the summer staff family at Dry Creek Camp on our annual Astros excursion in the midst of ten straight weeks of summer camp.

It's a Saturday game with the Cubs. The crowd is large—nearly a sellout.To understand this story, you must understand the configuration of Minute Maid Park. Its seating area is horseshoe-shaped. The open end of the shoe, the outfield, has few seats. Therefore, this ballpark is not conducive to that thing I hate: the crowd wave.

I've come for baseball—Craig Biggio and Jeff Bagwell

taking it to the hated Cubs. A crowd wave is a distraction and only for the novice fan, which most of our sixty-two staff are.

It starts with Thomas—as most things do.

Thomas is our most extroverted staffer. Tall, friendly, and sometimes goofy, he never meets a stranger and never backs down from a challenge. He's sitting in front of me when he stands and begins his wave.

It's an unrehearsed individual wave as he stands, flaps his arms, and yells. He's blocking my view of the game and I want to tell him to cool it, but resist.

Thomas is contagious. I've seen that work to the camp's benefit (and not at other times.) And Thomas is persistent. He repeats his one-man wave until his row joins in.

Soon our entire section of sixty-two enthusiastically start a wave. To our left, the grandstand ends, so there is only one way for the wave to travel and it quickly peters out among the other left field fans.

One shouldn't underestimate Thomas Bethke nor the power of youthful exuberance.

During this inning, Astros second baseman Jeff Kent is ejected for disputing a called third strike. This leads to a toe-to-toe-slobbering in your face argument between our manager, Jimy Williams, and the home plate umpire.

The manager is soon ejected and covers home plate with dirt before making his exit to the clubhouse.

The standing room only crowd—including our sixty-two young people—love it.

The Dry Creek staffers hoot and shout. They are into the game.

An inning later, one of them points down toward the field. "Hey look, there's Thomas… and Gary's with him."

The two staffers are standing behind the third base dugout among the expensive field level seats. How did they talk their way down there?

And you can guess what they are doing—leading a wave.

People who pay forty-five dollars to sit right behind

the dugout aren't interested in waves, but that doesn't deter Thomas.

Far away and high above, our sixty fans watch the two. After a while, the crowd responds and a series of waves ripple through the stadium.

To my amazement, the wave travels the circuit of the entire stadium. Even the open outfield area with its few standing fans joins in, and the loudest part of the wave occurs each time it passes by our fired-up crew of Dry Creek staffers.

Finally, we watch a security guard escort Thomas and Gary up the steps, out of the field level. On their return to our section, they receive a well-deserved hero's welcome.

The Astros won that day, but I've forgotten most of the game's details. I do know for sure the game's announced crowd because I wrote it down: 42,679.

I'll always remember the wave at Minute Maid Park, started by one determined and fun-loving teenager named Thomas who wouldn't quit.

Gary joined him. That's two. Then sixty more of their friends joined in and finally, thousands took part. Directly or indirectly, it affected 42,679. Whether they took part in the wave or just watched, they were affected by its energy.

It sure affected me. I have never forgotten it. I've told it hundreds of times to smiles, nods, and even tears from listeners, whether in Arkansas, Africa, or Alexandria.

Thomas' wave is an example of the ripple effect—how one person, with one passionate idea, can touch and change the world.

One of my spiritual heroes, Martin Luther, said this, "If you want to change your world, pick up a pen." He did just that, wrote his 95 theses—plus much more—and the world was never the same.

I doubt if my ripple effect will be world ranging, but I'd like it to be MINUTE-MAID-PARK in size. My job, like Thomas, is simply to send a ripple from my own spot in the park.

Each of us has our own ripple. It may be small, or may travel around the world. That's not important. The key is beginning your ripple right where you are and letting God spread it. He can do some amazing things if we will simply do our part and trust Him.

And when He does His part, the results—the math—are amazing.

Kind of like 1+2+62 = 42,267.

It's called the ripple effect.

Keep on Playing

Dry Creek Camp Tabernacle
Seven years ago

Someone leads the old man up onto the stage. I watch carefully, trying to figure out what is so unique about him. As they sit him in a chair by the piano, I realize, he's blind.

He pulls an object out of his bag. It's a tambourine.

The Singing Mackey Willis family joins him on the stage. The crowd of four-hundred men buzz in anticipation. They know there's going to be some fine singing in the Dry Creek Camp Tabernacle.

The Willis Family take the stage: Mackey, his wife Gayle, and their children T.J. and Heather.

I'm mystified by the blind tambourine man in the chair. When the music starts, he joins in. This old man is good—his rhythm and timing are perfect. He knows just when to be ready for one of Mackey's unique changes in time or improvisation. He is a wonderful addition to the already talented Willis family. The singing sounds extra good for there is nothing like hundreds of men singing in the Dry Creek Tabernacle. I always think, "This is what Heaven will be like!"

Being a drummer, I love the role of percussion in music. Listening to the tambourine man, it's obvious I'm in the midst of a master. If anything, his lack of sight enhances the play of his hand.

After thirty minutes of spirited singing, we dismiss to the dining hall for supper. I catch up with Mackey and ask, "Man, I like your tambourine player! Who is he?"

Mackey Willis looks at me with a quizzical smile and says, "I don't have any idea in the world who he is. I'd never seen him until he sat down by me on the stage."

This definitely arouses my curiosity, so I find the tambourine man. "You are good. It sounded as if you've played dozens of times with the Willis family. I couldn't get over your timing and clarity."

He grins and takes his instrument from under his arm, holding it up as he stares off into space. "Son, when I pick up this tambourine, God just takes over my hands. It's Him playing it, not me."

It was a wow moment. A simple statement that has vibrated in my heart—like his tambourine—since that day.

God takes over… It's Him playing, not me.

The tambourine man's statement is so true of how God wants to use the handiwork of our hands and hearts for His glory. We are all simply instruments in God's hands—ready and willing for use, but helpless and unable to strike a "rhythm" until His Hand and Spirit move upon us.

Any gift of the hands, as well as of the heart, is a special treasure given by God. Yes, we work on developing these gifts. Many times this skill is the result of hours and years of practice and sacrifice. But no one should ever forget that these "gifts of the hand" are a treasure from God, and it is only fitting that we express our appreciation and gratitude to Him.

℘

There is a famous story of another man with gifted hands—and also a gifted heart.

His name was Ignace Jan Paderewski and he was a famed Polish classical pianist of the last century.

On the night of this story, Paderewski was scheduled for a performance in Kansas City on a United States concert tour. The large sold out concert hall hummed with an air of anticipation as the well-dressed crowd filed into their seats.

About ten minutes before concert time, a person walked

out from the side of the stage. But it wasn't the grand master Paderewski who approached the spotlighted grand piano. Instead, it was a boy of about seven years old, wearing tennis shoes and jeans. With no fanfare, the boy simply went to the piano bench and took his seat.

Many in the crowd thought that maybe this was an opening act featuring a new prodigy of the keyboard. However, one attendee on the second row knew he was no prodigy. Her thoughts, as she looked at the empty seat beside her, were two-fold: How did my son get up on that stage? and What is he going to do up there?

The youngster at the piano did a strange thing. He raised both index fingers in the air before moving them to the keys. As he hit the first notes, a voice behind his mother whispered, "Chopsticks!"

The boy's playing was a typical seven-year-old's version of "Chopsticks." It was rough and several times he stopped, backed up, and restarted—but it definitely was "Chopsticks." Most were amused, but the mother blushed with embarrassment as her son had ruined the start of the performance of the world-famous pianist.

Just then, another figure appeared from the opposite wing. He also strode across the stage to the piano. It was the grand master himself. Watching, the boy's mother felt faint.

What happened next is an illustration that not only was Jan Paderewski a great pianist, but also a caring human being.

He leaned over behind the seated boy and whispered into his ear,

"Just keep playing . . . don't stop . . . keep playing."

With that, Paderewski began a beautiful two-handed accompaniment to "Chopsticks." The sight of the young boy beating out his two-fingered tune, as the great pianist reached around him playing along on each side of the keyboard was one never forgotten by those present that night.

And the duet was beautiful. It was music at its best. The ovation was long and loud as the two pianists, arm in arm, bowed to the crowd.

This story, one of my favorites, is a clear lesson of the work of our hands. We approach our instrument, whatever that may be, and begin our simple little two-fingered tune. Then our great God, if we allow Him, comes behind us and whispers, “Just keep playing… don’t stop… let me join you.”

And the resulting song is beautiful, touching, and memorable.

All because just like my tambourine-playing friend, we allow God to use and guide our hands.

So keep playing, don’t stop.

Just keep playing—

A Bright Light

Summer 1999

This story, from my days as Dry Creek Camp manager, still touches me when I read it and recall a wonderfully-terrible July Monday.

It's the time of evening I love best—the sun is going down, the shadows lengthen as another day slips by. In the oaks, the crickets and tree frogs tune up for their nightly duet.

Campers are scurrying to the Tabernacle. The excitement of a good day and the anticipation of the evening service can be felt in the air. It's just as real as the cool breeze blowing across the grounds. Everyone is full after a fine meal of chicken strips. Teenagers dressed in their new jeans laugh around the tree benches—the prime location for courting and friendship at Dry Creek Camp.

I rest in a nearby pavilion. As darkness approaches, I notice several outside lights aren't turned on. Irritation comes over me as I think, now who forgot to turn on the lights. My irritation is quickly pushed out of the way by sadness. The realization hits me that Brad won't be here to turn on the lights anymore.

Earlier this afternoon we buried Brad Robinson at Mt. Moriah Cemetery. He'd died two days earlier when struck by a drunk driver. The events of the last three days wash over me—the shock of losing Brad, the pain of sharing the news with his staff friends, the sorrow of seeing his grieving family—all play in an unending loop in my mind. My head pounds from the tears and emotion of the day.

Then I think about the sorrowful joy of the last three days and the strong faith of our staff. In spite of our grief, a deep peace fills my heart as I recall how God is faithful in all circumstances—even tragedy.

Only those who had lived this Monday could understand when I call it a "wonderfully terrible day."

I get up from my seat and begin turning on the lights. I guess it will be my job this evening. I wonder who will be the new "light" person at Dry Creek now that Brad is gone.

I think about the first time I saw Brad. He came in the spring of 1998 for a staffer try-out. I remember watching him get out of his truck dressed in overalls. His application had been impressive although he was only fifteen at that time. When I saw Brad there by his truck, I thought, this guy is not 15—he looks 20 years old. Brad Robinson possessed a physical and spiritual maturity that made him stand out.

That tryout weekend, Brad won our hearts with his hard work and big smile. When the weekend was over, our adult staff members said, "You better hire him, or we'll never talk to you again." And so began the special love affair between Brad Robinson and Dry Creek Camp.

That school year word kept filtering back about the tremendous revival occurring in Brad's school. It was linked to his contagious deep commitment to Jesus.

All of these memories come back as I flip on the outside lights. Walking by the laughing campers, my mind is a thousand miles away.

At the next light switch, Kristi Gallien ambles up sporting her famous smile. I've known her since she was born and have watched her grow into the special young woman she is. I truly love her like a daughter.

"Brother Curt, I'm in charge of the lights now. I need someone to make sure I know where they all are."

I step out of the darkness. "I'll show you while we walk." We relive the events of the day. I think about the picture of Brad at our home. He's dressed to kill with a huge smile on his face holding his cool sunglasses, leaving to pick up Kristi for the Prom. It's a photo fully revealing the personality of Brad

Robinson.

Kristi and I laugh and talk, through our tears, as we stroll to each light. As the last light is flipped on and Kristi walks away, I just stand for a while in the coming darkness. The lights illuminate various areas of the camp while others, away from the buildings, remained shrouded in night.

Then I think about the light of Brad's life . . . about how brightly it shined at Dry Creek, Mt. Moriah Baptist Church, LaCamp, Louisiana—and at Ray's Grocery and Hicks High School. I think about how his light shone. Even in death, his life witnessed as a bright light no drunken driver could snuff out.

And I'm confident that no amount of time will extinguish the bright light of Brad Robinson's life. He will live on in the hearts of all of us who love him. His witness will continue shining at Dry Creek long after those of us who love him are gone.

You see, when a young person sells out to Jesus, as Brad did, their witness and light burns for all eternity.

The words of Jesus sum it up best:

"You are the light of the world. A city on a hill cannot be hidden. Neither do people light a lamp and put it under a bowl. Instead, they put it on its stand, and it gives light to everyone in the house. In the same way, let your light shine before men, that they may see your good deeds and praise your Father in Heaven."

-Matthew 5:14–16

Postscript

As this book goes to print, there's an upcoming wedding in Dry Creek. Brad's beautiful sister, Brittany, is marrying my nephew, Brady Glaser.

I know the wedding will be a special day for all involved. Our two families have loved each other for over a decade.

But it will be a bittersweet day. I wish Brad could be there.

He'll be there in his own way as his influence and legacy live on.

You can't keep a bright light like his from shining.

Belum

Belum. It's a word from the sadness and devastation of post-tsunami Indonesia. In spite of the horrific stories told by the survivors, they often used this word.

Belum.

It's one of the most hopeful words I've heard.

When an Indonesian is asked a specific question, they qualify their answer in many ways and terms. For instance, the question, "Are you married?" may not get the "yes/no" answer a Westerner would give.

As expected, a married person would answer, "Ya" which means yes. Most likely, an unmarried Indonesian would answer, "Belum."

Ed, one of our team fluent in Indonesian and familiar with culture, pointed this out, "Belum simply means 'not yet'." Pronounced, "be-loom", it is a favorite word of Indonesians. Even the older lifelong bachelor or spinster would not answer this marital status question with "Tidak" ("No"), but instead they would answer with the eternally hopeful and optimistic, "Belum."

Several "Belum" questions come to mind:

"Have you ever been to America?"

"Belum."

I like a people that have that kind of outlook of life. This "No, I haven't done that/been there/seen that yet" attitude is pretty neat.

I began a list of questions that should be answered "Belum":

Have you seen the giant redwood trees of California?

"Belum."

Have you held a grandchild in your arms? "Belum."

Have you hiked the entire Appalachian Trail? "Belum."

Have you returned to Indonesia since your last trip? "Belum."

I like that word, "Belum."

It has an air of expectancy to it.

Hopefulness.

A holding out that it may—and shall—come to pass.

It must be spoken with a certain faith to it.

It is a good word for the follower of Jesus to carry with him/her. Above all peoples, we should be living with that hopeful, believing seed of faith in our heart and mind.

For such questions as:

Are you as close to Jesus as you wish to be?

"Belum."

Has that loved one you've prayed for come to the Lord?

"Belum."

Is God through with you at age________?

"Belum."

Have you been to Heaven?

"Belum."

Best of all, I like the "Belum" answer for the tough spiritual questions that stared us in the face on this trip after the tsunami. Questions such as, "Do you understand why God allowed this massive disaster and loss of life?"

"Belum."

I do not understand it and very likely will not on this side of Heaven's obscuring curtain. But in spite of my present "Belum," one day I will see this disaster, as well as our Louisiana "tsunamis" of 2005—Hurricanes Katrina and Rita, from the vast, infinite, eternal vista of God's will and plan.

Until then I'll follow the wise words of the great English preacher, Charles Hadden Spurgeon:

"God is too kind to be cruel

And too strong to be confused.

So when I cannot trace His hand,
I simply trust His heart."

Another important eternal question with that same one word reply is, "Have the precious people of Aceh Province turned to 'Isa Almasih,' or as I call him, Jesus the Messiah?" Once again, the answer is "Belum." But, it's a "Not Yet" with the firm knowledge that the seeds being planted are being faithfully watered and nurtured by the Master. The harvest, as always, is His and not ours.

Belum . . . It's a word I like.

The Mockingbird's Midnight Song

But at midnight Paul and Silas were praying and singing hymns to God, and the prisoners were listening to them
-Acts 16:25

It's the middle of another restless and sleepless night. Being exhausted both physically and mentally, yet unable to get the thing I need most—sleep—is deeply frustrating. So I wearily rolled out of bed. That's what all of the sleep books tell you to do when you have insomnia. Get out of bed and do something. Read. Eat a snack. Watch TV. Pray.

I've tried all of these night after night and very seldom do any of them work. My mind and heart are racing along at one hundred miles per hour. Nothing seems able to slow down the sadness and anxiety inside me.

On this particular night, I walk outside. It's about midnight, cloudy, and there is no moon. In the rural area where I live, very little outdoor light means it's really dark outside. Soon my eyes adjust to being outside. I've always loved country nights—looking at the stars, tracing the path of an overhead jet, and just soaking in the soothing sounds of a Southern night.

But in my depression and insomnia, my soul feels just as black as the darkness around me. I'm completely enveloped in it. I stand there, trying to concentrate and pray in the quiet darkness. I think back to the books I've read by those who've been depressed. These books all have something in common. They always describe their depression in terms of darkness, night, or blackness. One writer called it, "The black night of the soul." Author William Styron described it as "The black dog of despair." Winston Churchill, also a depression sufferer, called it "my black dog."

Tonight the silence is deafening. It's as if the night creatures—crickets, owls, frogs, and barking dogs—have found a hiding place to escape the darkness.

Then suddenly from the river birch tree in our driveway comes clear beautiful singing. It is a mockingbird. If you aren't from the South and haven't heard this bird, it is hard to describe its song. It is loud and is made up of about seven sequences of sounds - some stolen from other birds or nearby common sounds. In the classic book, Louisiana Birds, ornithologist George Lowery tells of a "mockingbird that so successfully imitated a dinner bell that it frequently caused the farm hands to come out of the field expecting their noon meal."

This midnight bird is a real singer who sits up high in the tree as the guardian of our yard. He sings—and sings loudly—with passion. To him, it doesn't matter that it is a dark moonless night when any respectable bird should be silently sleeping.

This mockingbird is singing even if it is midnight—even if it is dark—even if no one else hears his song. He chirps away for the simple pure joy of singing. Moreover, the fact that he has the entire sound stage to himself makes his song seem louder and fuller. It is the end of the opera and the great soloist is singing the aria—he needs no accompaniment. Any other sounds would only diminish the incredible beauty of this virtuoso solo.

This bird unknowingly gives me a great gift—I'm reminded of how a follower of God can sing—even in the darkness—even in tough circumstances.

And I'm reminded by this bird, and really by the God who created both him and his song, that I will get through this time of darkness. There is still hope for the restoration of joy. Even though now it seems I've lost my song, it is still deep within me. One day it will be sung loudly and joyfully once again.

I wish I could say my depression ended on that night, but that wouldn't be true. The mockingbird that sang at midnight was only one of a thousand steps on my road to restored health and joyful living. I firmly believe it was a gift from God just for me. It is a gift that I now pass on to you.

The gift of a mockingbird, in the darkness, singing at midnight.

"The Mockingbird's Midnight Song" is the title story from my fifth book. It contains essays and stories from a depressive episode I had in 2000.

It's my most fulfilling book, though it has sold the fewest copies of the seven. It has helped countless depression sufferers and their families.

To learn more about *The Mockingbird's Song*, visit www.creekbank.net.

Perfect Love

It's approaching 2 a.m. as I wearily turn into my driveway. My headlights reflect something strange: three boys on bicycles. I don't know any of them, so I roll down my window and ask what they're doing. They give me an ominous look and slowly pedal off.

Two o'clock in the morning is about four hours past my normal bedtime, but I'm coming in late from a baseball tournament with our son, Terry. Rainouts pushed our game to a late start and led to our early morning return home.

Driving into the carport, I wonder who the riders are and what they are up to at this time of night. Terry and I enter the house quietly, careful not to wake my wife DeDe and her visiting parents.

I quickly lock the garage door and think again about the nightriders out there. Terry runs water for a bath and I get a glass of milk, some cookies, and unfold the newspaper. As I sit on the couch, the dogs bark outside. I get the eerie feeling that the nightriders are still out there.

Suddenly, I hear the front door swing open. A chill goes up my spine as I expect to encounter one of the mystery riders coming down the hall with a weapon in his hand and malice on his mind. When I get the courage to check, the door is slightly ajar, and I see nothing in the blackness outside. Quickly I slam it shut, turn the deadbolt, latch the chain, and return shaken to my chair.

About one minute later a loud knock resounds off the front door. A muffled voice can be heard outside. Now I know for sure the nightriders are back. I go to the door and speak through it, "Who's out there?"

A voice responds, "Let me in."

Shakily I answer, "Who are you?"

The reply gives me the biggest scare of the night. My father in law responds, "It's Herbert. Open the door. You've locked me out!"

I quickly unlock the door to find my father in law standing there in his boxer shorts. He passes by me without a word, shaking his head, and quickly returns to bed, as I feebly attempt to explain.

I realize he had tried to get in the bathroom only to be blockaded by Terry who was enjoying his soaking bath after the game. Being a country man, he simply went outside on the porch. That's when I heard the door swing open and locked him out.

It's now nearly three o'clock. I return to my milk and cookies. In a few hours I'll be leaving for work—long before my father in law, Herbert Terry, arises.

Luckily for me, I didn't see him that day before he drove home.

My brother-in-law said his dad told him this upon returning home, "I thought I was going to have to give my name, rank, and serial number for Curt to let me back in the house." Then he added, "If you go down there, make sure you don't go out on the porch at night or you'll get locked out."

ℌ

I love to find a spiritual meaning in all of my stories. I bet you're thinking: he'll need to stretch it on this tale.

The next day it came to me: I had acted out of fear from the minute I saw those bike riders in my drive. Normally I'm not scared of much, but the late hour, my fatigue, and these strangers combined in putting me on the defensive, and the result was locking out my poor old father-in-law.

I then wondered how many times I've let fear lock others out of my life. How much love, how many friendships, and opportunities have I missed because of that dangerous emotion called fear?

There is such a thing as healthy fear. We all need a good dose of it. But more often than not, we are seized with the unhealthy variety—the kind that causes us to waver, doubt, and draw back.

That fearful fear strikes us in the dark, when we are tired, and when we are confused. It's the same situation and conditions that caused the disciples' fear on the raging Sea of Galilee. Even though the Creator of the universe lay in the boat asleep, they were fearful.

Living in the light of God's perfect love—that's how we cast out fear.

"Perfect love casts out fear."
- I John 4:18

The Sign Phantom

The sign said it all: "Wet Creek."

It all began in the spring of 1974, just prior to my graduation from high school. A rainy April had kept the local streams flooded in "Dry Creek."

One afternoon I went to the "Dry Creek" sign that informs the northbound traveler that they are entering our community. Over the "Dry" in Dry Creek I taped a white poster board sign saying "Wet." It now read, "Wet Creek." It was widely noticed and laughed at by everyone.

The Lake Charles American Press even ran a picture of the sign, commenting on our wet spring. The caption read in part, "The Highway Department is looking for the 'wag' that placed this sign, in defiance of regulations prohibiting the defacing of public signs." This caused me to lay low on my sign authorship. But for some reason, everyone in Dry Creek knew I'd done it.

Shortly after that, I placed another sign. This sign (to appease my humor-challenged highway department friends) was tied by hay string to the signposts below the Dry Creek sign. It read: Fun City, U.S.A.

This sign was meant as a final tribute to my soon-to-be former home as the prodigal son left "the sticks" for bigger and better things in college.

To understand this sign, you must know something about Dry Creek- both the stream and the community. To some, the name Dry Creek conjures up a small community in southwestern Louisiana.

The creek called Dry Creek is a small, muddy, steep-banked stream that meanders through the southeast corner of Beauregard Parish. It is not very wide, deep, or pretty. The Indians first named it. One old timer related as to how he'd been told the Indians really called it "Beautiful Creek," but the English translation got messed up and came out as "Dry Creek." Others claim the more traditional story of its name coming from the fact that the creek dries up in places during hot weather.

Then, there is the geographical area known as Dry Creek. It is simply an intersection of two highways. We have a post office, a church camp, a store, and some really good churches, but very little in the way of commerce or industry.

Many first time visitors will stand in the Post Office parking lot across from Foreman's Grocery and innocently ask, "Now, where is the actual community of Dry Creek located?" It's always fun to answer with a smile, "Friend, you're now standing right in the middle of downtown."

Not much exciting ever happened in our community. Therefore, to call Dry Creek, "Fun City, U.S.A." was to make light of what most anyone would agree is a quiet and boring community.

Later during the fall of 1974, I returned home from college, and was informed that "my signs" had continued appearing. My pleas of innocence were met with knowing smiles and winks. According to local folks, these signs, at the same location, continued poking fun at our community with such gems as:

"Hee Haw Filmed Here,"

"Airport Next Exit,"

and

"Famous for Nothing."

Even though no one believed my repeated denials, I had a good idea who the real sign phantom was. Later that year on another visit home, I saw a new sign and both the humor and handwriting gave it away. This sign related to the predicted "swine flu" epidemic that was of grave concern in 1975.

Doctors were advising many people, especially the elderly to receive vaccines. This new sign read:

"We ain't gonna give our hogs no flu shots."

I immediately knew my father was the sign phantom. Daddy, a lifetime highway department worker and church deacon, reluctantly admitted to me that he had continued the sign tradition.

When home, I'd always know when he was preparing a sign in the back room. The sound of his laughter and the squeaking of the magic marker announced a new sign was on the way.

We'd leave out late at night to put up the signs. His signs at this time continued on their themes of small town life and country values such as:

"Shop our Modern Mall,"
"It Sure Ain't Heaven,"
and
"Toll Bridge- One Mile Ahead."

Our longtime postmaster, Kat King, told of a stranger stopping at the post office for directions on avoiding the toll bridge. A female driver wanted directions to the nearby mall.

The signs continued and the legend of the Sign Phantom grew. I was still the number one suspect and no manner of denying could stop folks from believing it. All of my alibis about my being away from Dry Creek were not believed. At that time, I don't believe anyone even suspected my quiet and respectable dad.

Even though our community is small, many travelers pass through Dry Creek on their way to DeRidder or Bundick's Lake. The story of the signs at the Dry Creek Bridge spread throughout southwest Louisiana. Folks would stop in at the store commenting on the signs, and even complain about their absence, if no sign was up.

One lady from Westlake, who traveled our way weekly to her fishing camp, sent a letter addressed to the Dry Creek Chamber of Commerce. That anyone would think we had a Chamber of Commerce really tickled us. She commented how each week her entire family began leaning forward in their seats looking for the latest sign. She listed these as her favorites:

"We Have a Fine Sense of Rumor,"
"Crossroads to Nowhere,"
and
"First Annual Fire Ant Festival Next Week."

Many times the Sign Phantom commented on current events:
"Wedding Saturday Night Baptist Church- Bo and Hope"
(From the soap opera Days of Our Lives)
"Herb Lives in Dry Creek"
(From the famous Burger King Ad series)
"Killer Bees- Death Awaits You Here"
(As the dreaded killer bees approached Texas)
and "Protected by Patriot Missiles"
(During Operation Desert Storm).

Additional signs commented on social issues:
Gun control- *"Our wives, maybe. Our guns, never!"*
The lottery- *"Waiting for the lottery to make us all rich."*
Hunting- *"Do not shoot squirrels that wave or smile at you."*
Even professional wrestling- *"Don't tell us that wrestling is fake!"*

One of my personal favorites concerned an event from about fifteen years ago. In Washington State, three whales were trapped in a remote bay. Due to the shallow water at the bay entrance, the whales couldn't swim out. For several weeks, the national news media kept Americans informed on the plight of the whales. Volunteers from Greenpeace stayed at the bay attempting to help the whales. That same week, a sign appeared in Dry Creek:

"Help save the three gar trapped in Bundick's Lake."

Through the years people never believed it was my dad making these signs. I eventually began answering all inquiries with the plain truth, "It's my daddy doing them, not me." Usually they just laughed as if I was the world's greatest liar.

All in all, the hundreds of signs that were posted at the bridge were a commentary about our world during the 70s and 80s . . . and Dry Creek's (or more specifically, my dad's) reaction to it.

Thinking of the many signs over the years, I recall my all time favorite. An outsider driving through our community can best appreciate it:

"Don't laugh.
Your daughter may marry a Dry Creek Boy"

I bet my mother-in-law up in north Louisiana, and many other parents who've lost a daughter to a Dry Creek boy, can really appreciate that sign penned by the Sign Phantom of Dry Creek.

Sometimes during the early 1990's, the Highway Department came and moved the Dry Creek sign away from the bridge and closer to the community. They placed it right across from Turner's Grocery. That is when Daddy quit putting up his signs. He said the resident's dogs barked too much at this new location.

The legend of the Sign Phantom still lives on in the community of Dry Creek, Louisiana, better known as
"Fun City, USA."

A Father's Love

I've been to many graduations and heard my share of forgettable speeches. I've heard seniors sing everything from "Free Bird" to a memorable (not a good memory) version of "Stairway to Heaven" that would make Jimmy Page cut his hair.

But I'll never forget graduation night 2000 at the East Beauregard High football stadium. As I take you back to that night, you'll understand why.

My wife DeDe and I sit in the reserved seating section at the football stadium, awaiting our son Clint's high school graduation ceremony.

It's about fifteen minutes before the start when the cowboy walks onto the platform. Removing his hat, he leans into the microphone and blows on it. Yes, it's on … and he literally has the stage to himself, as well as the mike. Most people haven't even noticed him. Without accompaniment, he begins singing,

"Son, let me tell you about a father's love,
A secret that my father said was just between us.
You see, Daddies don't just love their children
Every now and then,
It's a love without end, Amen.
It's a love without end, Amen."

I faintly recognize the tune and remember it – It's the chorus of a George Strait song entitled, "A Father's Love."

Then about the same time, I recognize the singer on

stage—it's Greg Fontenot. Greg's son David is graduating tonight. David is a favorite of all of us with his wonderful smile and winning personality. He's an excellent athlete and a good student.

Although I don't know Mr. Fontenot extremely well, I've always enjoyed visiting with him. He is an expert in a trade that always brings respect in rural areas- he is an excellent welder. He is also a true country man, evidenced by the painting on the side of his welding truck;

"I ain't J.R. and this ain't Dallas…
but I can sure plow, plant, and hoe.
. . . and God bless."

By now Mr. Fontenot is singing the first stanza. He has now captured the attention of most of the crowd. Glancing around, some are sniggering; others sit in gape-jawed wonder. Someone behind me says, "I believe he's drunk." But watching closely, I can tell that Greg's not drunk, he's just singing a George Strait song from his heart.

I got sent home from school one day
With a shiner on my eye.
Fighting was against the rules
And it didn't matter why.
When dad got home I told that story
just like I'd rehearsed,
then stood on those trembling knees,
expecting the very worst…

And he said,
Son, let me tell you about a father's love,
A secret that my father said was just between us.
You see, Daddies don't just love their children
every now and then; It's a love without end, Amen.
It's a love without end, Amen.

Mr. Fontenot is singing this song well, which is not easily

done accapella. He has a fine singing voice that does justice to this country song. As Greg Fontenot begins the second verse, it is very evident that he has practiced and prepared for this night a long time. He continues,

When I became a father in the spring of '81,
There was no doubt that stubborn boy
was just like my father's son.
When I thought my patience had been tested to the end,
I took my daddy's secret and passed it on to him.

This time when he gets to the chorus, a few voices in the large crowd join in:

"It's a love without end, amen."

By now I'm thinking, I bet his son David is dying of embarrassment and wanting to hide. I think about my own three boys and remember the cardinal rule of raising teenagers: Don't embarrass me in front of my friends.

When Greg finishes the second stanza, he pauses and spits into a bottle he is holding. I think, I'd need a lot more than a dip of Skoal to have the courage to stand on a stage and do what he's doing.

Just as he begins the final climatic stanza, someone cuts off the microphone. I'm sitting close enough that I hear him exclaim, "Dang, if they didn't cut me off."

Someone sitting near us says, "Well, they should have let him go ahead and finish it if they'd let him sing that much." Another local music critic adds, "He was really doing pretty good and by the way, that third verse is the best one."

A smattering of applause comes from the audience, mixed in with many good-hearted shouts, and a few whistles. Greg Fontenot stands there as if they'll turn the microphone back on if he waits long enough. After what seems an eternity, he shrugs and walks off the stage onto the playing field.

Now, what happens next is why this is such a memorable story:

From across the field, where the graduates are assembled, comes a flash. It is a student running with his robe trailing behind him, holding onto his cap.

You've probably guessed whom it is running—it's David Fontenot, running full tilt toward his dad. He's running across the same field where last fall, wearing number 80, he ran so many times with the football.

He runs to his dad and embraces him warmly. I can read his lips repeating, "Thank you, thank you." I now realize we have seen a special gift from a father to his son. An act from a father that will help "weld" their souls together for the rest of their lives.

I realize that this country father understands about more than one type of welding—a welding of human hearts.

Only later do I learn that Greg Fontenot had been planning this song all year. He had even asked the principal for permission to sing before the ceremony started. Mr. Cooley had kind of put him off and probably forgot about it until on graduation night when Greg sang his first solo.

During the coming days, I enjoyed sharing the story of David and his dad. I also think of all of the ways a man can give his "blessing" to a son or daughter.

We see this in several Biblical stories. Each one unique but conferring the same story, "You are my child and I see something very special in you. I am proud of you."

By far the most powerful Biblical example of a father's blessing is at Jesus' baptism. As Jesus begins his public ministry at age thirty, he chooses to be baptized in the Jordan River by his older and more well-known cousin, John.

Jesus, being the perfect Son of God, did not need baptism for repentance of sins- because He was sinless. He sought baptism as an example of obedience. John the Baptist even initially refused to baptize Jesus, famously stating that he was not worthy to even untie Jesus' sandals.

After John relented and the newly baptized Christ came up out of the water, the scriptures state, "The Holy Spirit came down like a dove and a loud voice spoke from Heaven: 'This is my beloved Son in whom I am well pleased'."

The statement above was one of a father blessing his son. Jesus needed to hear that from His Father. Jesus, being perfect and having existed with God from before eternity, still needed those words of approval.

The excellent book, *The Blessing* by John Trent, shares numerous accounts of the importance of fathers and their words and actions of approval and blessing on their children.

I started thinking about my own father and how he gave "the blessing" to me. My father came from a very good family, but they weren't much on flowery words. Because of that he was never really comfortable sharing, "I love you." with us. But I never felt shortchanged one bit. There was never one moment in my life where I ever doubted the love of both my mom and dad.

Daddy had many ways of saying, "I'm pleased and proud of you." Here's how I know: I became camp manager at Dry Creek when I was thirty-six. Not too long after that a friend related, "I was at a meeting where your dad sang. He introduced himself as 'Curt's father' and called you 'his hero'."

Over and over during the last decade of his life he would say that about me. Many times he said it in front of me. Words cannot describe how much it meant. It amazed me that the man who was always my hero thought of me as his. That motivated me, and still does, to be the father, husband, and man I should be.

Here's a final thing about my dad's "blessing." It released me from ever feeling as if I must be exactly like him.

Since his death, I've heard repeatedly, "Son, you've got some big shoes to fill." I always smile and agree with them, but I've never felt like I must fill my dad's shoes. As great of a man as he was, he gave me the freedom of being my own man—allowing me to make my own decisions and choose my own path.

That's one of the things about the blessing—it brings

freedom and release.

Correspondingly, my mother has given me this same blessing for all of my fifty plus years. I have two wonderful younger sisters whom I love dearly, but being the only son, I've always been extremely close to my mother.

I often leave this message on Mom's answering machine. "Hey, this is your favorite son calling." Her comment over the years has been consistent, "It wouldn't matter if I had other sons, you'd still be my favorite."

My mother is the fairest and most even-handed mother and grandmother in the world. I know she would love another son no more or no less than me, but those words—my favorite son—still warm my heart. I believe Jesus' heart was warmed in the same way when His Father said, "This is my beloved son, in whom I am well pleased."

Yes, the blessing…

Coming from a father's love….

It's priceless…..

Finally, Greg Fontenot's graduation song, which really started off this long spiel, had a wonderful third verse. Even though Greg never got to sing it on that May night, it bears repeating. It tells of the best blessing of all, our Heavenly Father's love for us:

Last night I dreamed I'd died and stood
Before those pearly gates,
When suddenly I realized there must
be some mistake.
If they know half of the things I've done
they'll never let me in.
Then somewhere from the other side I
heard these words again,

And He said,
"Son, let me tell you about a father's love,
A secret that my father said was just between us.

You see, Daddies don't just love their children every now and then,
It's a love without end, Amen.

…Yes, it's a love without end, Amen.
A Father's Love
A love without end,
Amen.

Best Seat in the House

October 19, 1996
"A pine knot fire crackles in front of me; a cool breeze rustles foliage that is just going crimson and gold. A half moon glistens overhead and I am finishing my evening meal with hot cocoa and a chocolate bar. Somewhere to the north, fifty to sixty thousand people are packed into Yankee Stadium for the first game of the World Series. They paid more, but I have the better seat by far."

-Copied from a trail journal at Blue Mountain Shelter on the Ouachita Trail in Central Arkansas.

I love the fine prose from that unnamed hiker in Arkansas.

As you've noticed if you've made it this far through *Deep Roots*, many of my stories relate to the outdoors and nature.

In the woods is where I feel closest to God. There is something about being among nature that causes even a non-believer to think that there is too much order for this to be by accident. When I'm outdoors walking and listening, stories of nature and our Creator just seem to come.

Last spring when it was still cool and the mosquitoes, redbugs, and ticks had not yet become a nuisance, I was on a late evening walk. As I approached Crooked Bayou, the stream along which my family's homestead is, I sat down to watch the approaching darkness in the swamp. It was quiet and seemed as if the whole world had taken a temporary vow of silence.

Suddenly a far off owl called.

Sitting on the creek bank, I cupped my hands over my mouth for my best owl imitation, and was happily surprised when the owl returned my call. We continued our "conversation" and soon he neared to investigate the trespasser on his personal property.

To the west, deeper in the swamp, another owl answered. We now had owls "in stereo." With each series of hoots, the first owl got closer to where I was sitting. The second owl called from its original location.

When my owl friend hoots again, I strain my eyes looking up in the surrounding beech trees to catch a glimpse of him. I know the direction he's calling from, but cannot spot him. Owls have an uncanny skill in throwing their voices.

Finally, it flies into the tree directly above me. It flaps its broad wingspan before settling on a limb.

There is still enough light to see the owl's silhouette. I sit quietly not wanting to scare it away. The owl and its partner to the west continue calling back and forth.

Just like the unknown October hiker from that Arkansas shelter, I have "the best seat in the house." I've got a front row box seat for the evening hoot owl concert.

As the dueling owls continue their chatting, I detect a more excitable song on the end of their calls. Dr. George Lowery, in *Louisiana Birds* states, "… hoots are followed by a long drawn out weird scream that is enough to chill the bones of the uninitiated."

I agree about the spookiness of this scream. I don't know exactly what it means – whether it is a challenge to fight, or an invitation to visit. Their mocking spooky calls end with my nearby owl flying toward the west and the other owl flying to meet it.

It's dusk-dark now and I cross a small log over the creek, headed back from the swamp to higher ground and my truck. It's a good feeling being out in the woods. No time schedule, no interruptions … just having the best seat in the house – a front row seat at the evening hoot owl concert.

Postscript

The following is from a letter by Ryan Collie, a US Marine serving in Iraq, to his mother:

I wanted to close this letter by sharing a story with you that Bro. Curt wrote in one of his books. It's called "The Best Seat in the House."

The story was of a hiking trip he took on the Ouachita Trail in Central Arkansas. During the hike he stopped at one of the shelters to take a breather and shared a story from a trail journal. The entry was about a man missing the first game of the World Series but having "the best seat in the house" in the mountains.

"The night I read that story, I saw one of the most beautiful Iraqi sunsets of my life and realized that I too, for once, had 'The best seat in the house.'

And as much as I've missed home, I've enjoyed every second here. After all, everyone at home was probably doing the same old things they do every day, and here I am getting a chance to see a sunset I might have never seen that was probably 'rained out at home'."

Christmas Jelly

"The only true gift is a portion of yourself."
-Ralph Waldo Emerson.

Of all my holiday gifts, Christmas jelly is always my favorite.

Each year I receive this special gift from a very special lady in my life. Before I share what Christmas jelly is, let me share about the special person who gives it each year.

Eleanor Andrews is my neighbor in Dry Creek. All of my life she has lived in the same house along Highway 113. Her house is easy to spot as it has the prettiest yard in our community. Her beautiful garden, flowers, and shrubs are examples of her love of gardening.

Mrs. Andrews is more than just my neighbor and a lover of flowers. She is also my all-time favorite teacher. Mrs. Andrews taught fifth grade at Dry Creek High School and later at East Beauregard High. She taught practically every young person in Dry Creek for a period of a quarter century.

Eleanor Andrews was from the "Old School." She was stern and took no gruff or lip off any student. Everything was rigid and "down the line" in her classroom. There was no doubt that she was captain of the ship. She possessed a stare (made complete with her tongue tucked firmly in her cheek) that would stop a charging grizzly bear in its tracks.

Her reputation preceded her, and she was just as strict as the older kids on the bus had described her. Sitting in her fifth grade class, I also saw something else: Beneath that gruff exterior were warm smiling eyes. She loved watching students learn and leading young people into new knowledge. During that year, 1967, she became my favorite teacher. And now over thirty years later, she still is.

Now let me get back to that Christmas jelly. Eleanor Andrews has been retired for many years and is much older and frailer than when she ruled the fifth grade. Because of her health she doesn't venture out much anymore. She lives alone surrounded by her flowers and memories of a life filled with teaching and touching lives.

Each year a few weeks before Christmas I receive a phone call from her, telling me to "to drop by her house." I know that the best present of the season is now complete—Christmas jelly is ready.

Before going I cut one of the Christmas trees from my farm. I tagged it weeks earlier, carefully choosing one that would meet her exacting standards. After loading it in my truck, I nervously drive to her home, hoping she will approve of my tree. Once again I feel as if I'm in the fifth grade waiting to hand in an important assignment.

Entering her living room, I'm greeted with that special smile I've known over the years. Always when I'm in her presence she makes me feel as if I'm the most important person in the world—that's why she's always been my favorite teacher.

She thrusts a basket of eight jars into my arms, each filled with homemade jelly. There are all of my favorites: muscadine, mayhall, even crabapple. Included are several jars of hot pepper jelly, and to top it all off, a Ziploc bag of chocolate "Martha Washington's."

I look at this assortment of homemade jelly and my mouth waters thinking about all the biscuits it will top off during the coming year. Oh, the joys of homemade jelly. As Mrs. Andrews happily examines her Christmas tree, she insists on paying for it. I laugh. "No way. The best deal I ever make is trading a tree for the best home-made jelly in Dry Creek."

I leave with my arm load of jelly jars. As I get in my

truck, I think about the art of giving. I look at the colorful decorated jars of jelly and am once again reminded of what Christmas is truly about. It is all about giving—giving of ourselves as we share what we have. I'm so glad to live in a place where gifts like Christmas jelly abound.

Like so many of my mentors and teachers, Eleanor Andrews is no longer alive. What would I give to sit in her living room again, hearing her warm laughter, and eating one of her chocolate treats.

Christmas is about enjoying and being grateful for our many gifts. Be sure to spend time with the special people in your life.

Two Men—One Word

This is the story of two men, and the one word that describes them.

They are two very different men—from different races, backgrounds, cities, and contrasting lifestyles.

As far as I know, they've never met, but in my mind their lives will always be united due to the word.

The word is compelled, and rather than dryly defining it, let me tell their stories. Then you'll understand why these two compelled men are forever linked in my mind and heart.

After Katrina, there were doers who didn't wait around for permission from FEMA or the Red Cross or the mayor or government. They simply did what needed doing and "got-'er-done."

They had a "W.I.T." attitude: Whatever it takes.

Whatever it takes to get the job done.

First of all, there's Carl.

Carl Lightell is one of the real heroes of New Orleans.

As Katrina approached and his city emptied, he made a decision. He decided to stay. Sending his wife Mamie off, he began getting ready for the storm.

In Carl's West Bank neighborhood of Terrytown, heavy rains always cause flooding. So during regular downpours, Carl and another neighbor would clear the storm drains of debris. The entire neighborhood appreciated these men and their unofficial jobs as storm drain cleaners.

With Katrina approaching, Carl's helper had evacuated New Orleans, so the job was left to him. He wasn't sure if cleaning the storm drains would keep the hurricane's waters out of his neighborhood, but he planned on finding out.

As Carl later told me, "I felt that I must stay. It was my job—my home."

He may or may not have known about the word "compelled" but he lived it.

It's a word that means "driven" or "forced." It is an action word where one is swept along—nearly in spite of themselves—to do something.

This is why Carl stayed to protect his home and neighborhood—he felt compelled. He didn't stay to loot—or wait on the government to rescue him. He stayed because he felt compelled.

When Katrina hit with its full fury, Carl went out in the driving rain clearing out the drains. Several times it looked as if the water would get in the homes of the neighborhood, but it didn't—thanks to Carl. And the next day when the levees broke, Carl's area fortunately was unaffected by the rising water.

In the days after the storm, he stood on his porch as the looters roamed through his neighborhood. He didn't have a weapon. He simply stood there with arms crossed letting the armed young men know he was here and wasn't going anywhere.

A week after Katrina is when I first met Carl. He had joined Mamie at the City of Hope shelter in Dry Creek. He was a quiet wiry black man who avoided the crowds at the shelter. Instead, he went quietly about his business. It was evident in the weeks he was here that he liked working. He'd worked hard all of his life and didn't intend changing now. He was always busy with helping at the camp. As I watched him and heard his story, he became one of my heroes.

It would embarrass Carl to know he was mentioned for simply "doing what he had always done." But Carl's story and his role needs telling … for every looter carrying a big screen TV out of a store, there were ten Carl Lightell's staying for the right reasons. For every victim screaming at the government or FEMA, there were the "Carl's of the world" picking up the load and carrying it.

A man who felt compelled to stay. Who did what he could in his neighborhood—cleaning out the storm drains.

Then there is the story of another compelled man—Tom Dunville.

Tom didn't stay in New Orleans. He went.

I've known Tom for ten years. He is a wonderful artist and one of the nicest guys I know… when he is sober. Tom has fought a lifelong battle with alcohol. Sometimes with the help of the Lord, he has won. At others, the bottle has had the upper hand. But sober or drunk he is my friend, and I love him like a brother.

Tom re-surfaced in Dry Creek on the day the levees flooded New Orleans. He and his son-in-law Tim Evans watched on TV as New Orleans went under water. Tom, Tim, and four other buddies in the small town of Westlake decided to do something about it.

But first they needed a boat. Tom remembered that our pastor, Don Hunt, had a fishing boat. So they came to Dry Creek, borrowed our pastor's flat-bottomed aluminum boat and headed out.

State police stopped them at the edge of New Orleans. Tom said they told "a little white lie" convincing the officers that they were part of the official Wildlife and Fisheries Department caravan. "We just got separated from the rest of the rescuers."

Once inside New Orleans there was no stopping them. They put the boat in at the 17th Street Canal that separates Orleans and Jefferson Parish. By going through the levee breaches they were able to reach areas of the city with the deepest water. For the next four days they rescued people from rooftops and the second stories of buildings.

Tom said they never saw a uniformed official in the first three days. Civilians did the initial stages of the rescue. Tim Evans and a Baton Rouge Marine, Mason Crawford, commandeered (my favorite post-hurricane word) a one-ton semi truck and five flat bottom boats. They used them to haul people off rooftops to Interstate 10.

Now if you saw Tim, Tom, and their crew you'd say they look like a pretty rough bunch. But if you were stranded on a roof for three days, you'd see their heart long before you looked at their hair or dress.

When describing his decision to go to New Orleans, Tom Dunville had a simple but deep explanation, "After I saw the flooding, desperation, and great need I just felt compelled to go."

Once again, that word compelled. Tom and his friends saw a great human need and something deep within forced him, in compassion, to take action and go.

I could add numerous examples of this "compelled philosophy" we saw during our two hurricanes, but I'll stop with Carl and Tom.

May we remember that we saw the best of most folks during this time. When crisis comes there always seems to be several groups of people. Some are concerned and will take action if given permission. Others choose to sit on the sidelines and correct or criticize every action of those on the field.

Then there are the compelled. They see a need and their heart will not let them sit back or criticize—they must act or die. That is what happens when the two "C" words of compassion and compelled connect. Actions and results, aimed at helping people, result.

It's when we see the human race at its best.

A compelled person grabs what is at hand and goes to work. While others turn away from the challenge, they choose to take action.

Like Carl, they choose to stay and take care of the needs at home.

Like Tom, they see a need in a strange place, and feel compelled to go.

It's a life philosophy of "getting-'er-done."

That doesn't need a hurricane to shine.

That "compelled" way of life.

The complete story of the Tom Dunville "fishing expedition" appeared in the "Lake Charles American Press" edition on Sunday, September 11, 2005.

Henry

Author's note:

What does a story about a young tsunami survivor have to do with a book about the Louisiana Piney Woods? Here is my short list answer: Henry's story is about heart and courage, noteworthy qualities worth celebrating in any culture at any time.

About 10,000 miles from my Louisiana home is the Indonesian island of Sumatra. I do believe part of my heart is still there. I left it in the dark brown hands of a young man named Henry.

I met Henry among the ruins of his hometown of Lampuuk. It had been over eleven weeks since the tsunami, and Henry lived in a tent not far from the only remaining building in Lampuuk, the local Mosque. Every other building in this once bustling village of 10,000 was flattened.

A handsome twenty-year-old with an infectious smile and wonderful personality, Henry quickly became the favorite among all of our medical team. He had an excellent command of English as well as the widely spoken Basra Indonesian and local Achenese dialect.

As we began setting up our medical clinic at Lampuuk, Henry came out of his tent to greet us. He seemed to be the official goodwill ambassador of the village. Henry had a cheerful, contagious smile that said, "I've been through a lot, but I'm still standing."

He also possessed a great pride that led him to question every American visitor with the same inquiry: "Have you ever met a president of your United States of America?"

My reply was an honest, "No."

Our new Indonesian friend broke out into a wide grin and proudly said, "Well, I've shook hands with two of your presidents right here where we are standing. I visited with your presidents: Bush senior and Clinton three weeks ago. We talked for over thirty minutes." I could easily envision Henry schmoozing with our two leaders on their visit earlier in February. I have no doubt he held his own in conversation with both of them.

I asked Henry to show me where his house had been. We walked through the rubble and debris of what had once been a thriving village. In every direction the only reminders of human habitation were the cement foundation slabs swept clean by the waves.

He stopped at a clean-swept concrete slab. "This was our home. On the morning of the earthquake, everyone ran outside looking around. My dad and younger brother were with me. The shaking continued and was accompanied by a great deal of shouting and running around. When the message was passed around about the receding ocean and fish, many folks ran toward the ocean. For some reason, my father, brother, and I did not run. We simply stood there wondering what was next."

He pointed toward the ocean. "It was probably fifteen minutes after the quake when we first heard it. You could hear the roar of the wave before you could see it. When we saw it coming, everyone ran. My father and brother were behind me as we fled for our lives toward higher ground."

As Henry spoke, he pointed to a grove of tall coconut trees about one-half mile away. "That is where I was headed. The wave, it was actually three waves traveling together, was moving about thirty kilometers per hour—slow enough to outrun for a short distance. Looking back I saw my father and brother trailing farther behind me. When the wave washed over the Mosque it was about there on its side." Henry pointed to a spot about thirty feet high on the Mosque wall. Although it had stood, the entire Mosque was gutted and the stairwells had been torn away.

He pointed toward the grove of trees. "The last I saw of my father and brother was when they were overtaken by the water. Eventually the water reached me and I frantically tried to run in it, and then swim. The debris being pushed along hindered free movement. I passed out and later awoke on higher ground near the trees. I have no idea how I escaped."

Henry's story, as well as the way he so dispassionately told it, touched me. It was as if he was describing a normal event or the happenings on another planet. I wondered how many times he had related his tale, but just because he told it without much emotion did not mean it was not burned deep into his soul. Here was a young man, the age of my sons, who had lost everything.

In the coming days we spent a great deal of time with Henry as he traveled with us to the clinics. He was great help with the older patients who spoke mainly Achenese. He would "interpret for the interpreters" as he translated the patient's symptoms to the interpreters, who then translated it into English for our doctors.

I think of the difficulty of starting the renovation of an area so utterly devastated. Then I think of Henry and his optimism that not even the storm could wash away. This same deep inner resolve was evident and indicative of the many Achenese people we met and grew to love.

The task of rebuilding northern Sumatra, just like our task has been in New Orleans and throughout our part of Louisiana, is completely overwhelming. In Lampuuk that day very little rebuilding had been done, even after three months. How will they even know where to begin?

Then I think about the young people I met there—Henry and his wonderful smile and "can do" personality. I see the faces of Raihail and her student nurses. I think of Saeed our driver and Dedek, a young Indonesian who worked with us. Then there is Jenni, a vibrant young Indonesian from another part of the country, casting her lot with these Achenese in rebuilding their lives and cities. In addition, there will be countless others who will answer the call of rebuilding their cities and country.

The new Lampuuk will be different, just as the new New Orleans will not be the same. And as always, it will be young minds, and strong hearts, and innovative minds leading the way.

When Hurricane Katrina struck Louisiana, I began hearing from these Indonesian friends named above. In their e-mails and letters, they expressed deep concern and empathy for the plight of my home state. Without exception, they called the hurricane, "your tsunami."

I told them that as horrible as Katrina and later Rita were, they couldn't compare to what I'd seen on their island. I recalled silently standing at a huge freshly plowed field where 25,000 tsunami victims were buried in a mass grave.

Nothing that had happened in Louisiana could approach that.

But my lasting memory of the tsunami area is not the cement slabs and mass graves. It's the faces of the young people—the ones who are rebuilding their villages, cities, and countries—which are burnt into my mind.

Just like the smiling face of my friend Henry and his village of Lampuuk.

Two years after being in Sumatra, I met one of those ex-presidents, George H.W. Bush in Alexandria. As he talked about the tsunami, his voice choked and tears welled in his eyes.

I understood fully. He had stood on the deserted beach at Lampuuk, and just like everyone else, he was changed by it.

A Homeless Lady

And Jesus said, when you have done it unto the least of these my brethren, you have done it unto me.
- Matthew 25:40

When the teenager saw me, he sprinted over. "Bro. Curt, there's a homeless lady inside the Tabernacle, and she won't let any of us help her."

"A homeless lady in Dry Creek?" I let the shock register on my face.

A knot of youth joined him, assuring me it was true. One of them grabbed my arm and led me toward the Tabernacle. Nearing, I could hear the loud music of the band and hundreds of voices singing, "Open the eyes of my heart, Lord. Open the eyes of my heart."

At the main door, a woman burst out, nearly knocking me down. She wore ragged layers of clothing, carried several plastic shopping bags stuffed with who knows what, and looked as if she was trying to escape from something or someone. Right behind her were several other campers desperately trying to stop her. As she swept by, I futilely grabbed at her elbow. In spite of how quickly she moved by, I could detect her body odor and the unmistakable mix of mildewed clothing and mothballs.

I noticed that she was hugging a new Bible against her breast and carrying a bottle of water in her other hand. In the Bible I could see a $10 bill sticking out. Ignoring my plea to stop, she brushed by and headed toward the highway. Deep inside, I was happy to see her headed that direction and away from the camp.

Several of these "would-be Good Samaritan" campers walked briskly imploring her to stay. The remaining teens begged me to stop her so they could give her money, food, and encouragement. Several of them had tears in their eyes as they implored me to "do something."

Watching her disappear along Highway 113, I told them: "We can't help this lady. She doesn't belong here at our camp among a bunch of godly teens." I thought the campers were going to jump me! Their faces registered a mixture of disgust, pain, and disappointment in my callous remarks.

Then I told them the truth. "That lady was a test for all of you. She's not really a homeless lady. In fact she lives nearby in Ragley. She had hidden her nice car down the road and walked onto the campgrounds. I had asked her to come dressed as a homeless lady as a test to see how our campers would react. Each of you passed the test—in fact, you passed it with flying colors. We've talked all week about ministering in the name of Jesus to hurting folks. You went out and put that talk into action with your concern. The gifts of money, bottled water, a Bible, and your concern were good and right."

As I told the whole story about this "spiritual speed trap," I thought one of the girls was going to hit me with her Bible! I explained how the first time two years previously, when this lady showed up at a camp weekend retreat, she was unknown to our workers. Staff member Dwayne Quebedeaux kept trying to help her until she finally whispered under her breath, "Hey man, quit pestering me. I'm not really a homeless lady. I'm doing this to see what reaction the ladies at this retreat will have. Give me some room."

I reassured our teen staffers how proud I was of them. The fact that the sight of another person in need did not drive them away, but instead stirred their hearts to action was good, right, and compassionate. Caring hearts will respond not just with words, but also with deeds and action. That is why the homeless lady was carrying all types of gifts given as tokens of the concern of these campers.

Later that evening I called our "homeless lady." On the phone, I told her, "I'm nominating you for an Academy Award. You were authentic, even down to the smell!"

She replied, "I thought some of those kids were going to knock me down they were so helpful!" I thanked her for taking time to "show a sermon" and test the hearts of these precious campers.

As I mentally reviewed the aggressive compassion of our campers I thought of this quote, "She is such a good friend that she would throw all of her friends in the water just for the sake of being able to fish each of them out."

Pondering over it later, I wondered why some campers were moved to instant action at the sight of this homeless lady while others, who may have also been concerned, took no steps in getting involved.

There is only one word that can explain the actions of the teenagers who "attacked" the homeless lady with love: Compassion.

Compassion. It's another of my favorite words.

An action word that moves beyond concern, even caring.

Yes, compassion—the beautiful word that our campers showed Dry Creek's only "homeless lady" on that memorable day.

When he (Jesus) saw the crowds, he was deeply moved with compassion for them, because they were troubled and helpless, like sheep without a shepherd
-Matthew 9:36

Suzie Q

Somewhere in China
October 2003

I'll never see her again on this earth.

Although I often think of her, I never even knew her name. She was a courageous brave Chinese Christian—one of the bravest people I've met.

I'm certain we will meet in Heaven and believe I'll recognize her by those dark unforgettable eyes.

We didn't talk because she knew no English and I don't speak Mandarin Chinese. In addition, our meeting was brief because it placed her in great danger. That danger was because of the packages she carried.

I was one of four backpackers in this Chinese city. We'd been instructed to meet a woman this morning at the local train station. She would find us because there was no way we'd ever find her in this river of Chinese faces. Four tall and pale Americans carrying backpacks wouldn't be hard to spot in rural China.

The train station was so "Asian": stacked with people. We stood outside in the surging crowd—all whom were trying to get through the two doors leading into the staging area.

Finally, we saw her—her nervousness was a dead giveaway. Following behind her were two porters each shouldering a long bamboo pole with bags on each end. Approaching us, her eyes darted back and forth nervously. This might seem like a game for us, but it was dead serious for her.

She handed our leader Randy a cell phone, train tickets, our four bags, and directed us toward the crowded station entrance.

Before leaving, she looked deeply into each of our eyes. Her earlier look of nervousness was replaced by one of grim determination. Those eyes seemed to say, “OK, I’ve done my part. It’s time for you to do yours. It’s worth the risk I’m taking to tell others about the difference Jesus Christ has made in my life.”

The bags she gave us contained DVDs of the Jesus Film in the heart language of her minority people group. For the first time they would see—and hear—the story of Jesus in their native tongue.

In the coming days as our team hid the film in woodpiles, under rocks, and in the rows of the corn and sugar cane fields, I often thought of this brave girl with the bright determined eyes. She had put herself in great danger delivering these packages. If we Americans were caught with these materials, we would be unceremoniously escorted out of the country.

On the other hand, if this young Chinese woman was caught, the repercussions would be serious. She most probably would face a stiff jail sentence as well as long-term persecution.

Backpacking the countryside, we often talked about this woman. Our brief encounter had left a lasting impression on us. We finally gave her a name, “Suzie Q.” From then on that was how we knew her.

Suzie Q. Our brave Chinese contact.

We walked the fields and roads of rural China hiding our precious packets. Our goal was this: We wanted them found, but not before we cleared out. After distributing the packets over a three day period, we were instructed by phone where to meet Suzie Q for a second shipment.

Our second rendezvous was at a bus station in a large city. As our taxi pulled to the curb, Suzie Q stood beside four bags. We noticed several policemen standing nearby. The sight of four Americans picking up the bags must have aroused their curiosity, but no one questioned us. In fact, one of the police officers directed us to the correct line for our bus.

Suzie Q urged us toward the terminal doors. When we turned, she was gone. It was our last time to see her.

This time we headed north to another minority people group. These new packets were in a different dialect from our earlier stash.

We never saw her again.

On our way home, we stopped in Hong Kong. Being curious about Suzie Q, we asked our contact about her. She smiled. "She is a vibrant twenty-year-old Christian who sells hair combs on the streets of her city. She's a brave and deeply committed follower of Jesus, regardless of the risk or cost."

But our contact wouldn't reveal the Chinese woman's real name. So she'll always be, at least in this life, Suzie Q.

When we do meet again—on the other side—she'll know my name, and I'll finally know hers. Until then, she is "Suzie Q," the brave young Chinese woman with the bright unforgettable eyes …

Postscript

Jen, the Chinese missionary who coordinated our trip from Hong Kong, later sent an email: "We returned to one of the villages where your team had hidden Jesus Films, and discovered fellow believers there. When we inquired as to who had brought them the message of Jesus, they shrugged, 'No one came. We found DVDs with the story of Jesus, watched, and came to believe'."

The new Chinese believers were incorrect on one thing. Someone did come. A long list of someones linked together to get the DVDs to a cornfield in rural China.

They were all important, but none more important than the strongest—and bravest—link in that long chain: a courageous Chinese woman named "Suzie Q."

Stuck on Devil's Tower

"Hey y'all, watch me do this."
-Proverbial last words of a redneck

. . . I'm sure it seemed like a good idea at the time. It was October 1, 1941 when daredevil George Hopkins did something incredibly stupid: He parachuted onto the top of Wyoming's Devil's Tower.

Recently while visiting this impressive national monument, I read about Hopkins' stunt. He did it for attention and got much more than he had bargained for! His Plan A went fine. He guided his parachute down onto the semi-flat rocky top of the Tower, which is about the size of two football fields.

But Plan B went awry when the same plane that he jumped from failed to properly drop the long rope and climbing stakes he planned in using for his descent down the 865-feet-high volcanic plug.

So, George Hopkins was stranded atop Devil's Tower. For the next week, Americans followed his saga. Finally, after six days a group of experienced climbers ascended the mountain and brought poor George down.

This story from Devil's Tower is a good example of starting good, but not having a rehearsed plan to finish well. This is true in our lives as well. Steve Farrar's excellent book, Finishing Strong addresses this subject for men. It's a must-read book that I recommend highly.

The story of being stuck atop Devil's Tower also has another spiritual application: When we land atop sin in our lives, it is a lot easier and fun landing on it than getting off.

The Bible speaks of the temporary “pleasure of sin for a season” in Hebrews 11:25.

An old adage expands on it:

“Sin will take you farther than you want to go,
keep you longer than you want to stay,
and cost you more than you want to pay.”

Devil’s Tower might be a good place to land, but not to stay. The journey there looks great, once you arrive it is barren, rocky, waterless, and unmercifully hot.

It’s a whole lot harder getting off Devil’s Tower than getting on.

Be careful what you jump for. It’s not always easy to get off!

Don’t believe me?

Just ask an old daredevil named George Hopkins.

92 Dry Holes

I probably would have given up long about dry hole number sixteen.

But Amon Carter didn't and that was the reason I stood in the wonderful Ft. Worth, Texas museum bearing his name. The tour guide told a story that impressed me as much as any of the art: Amon Carter, a West Texas oil wildcatter, drilled 92 dry holes before he struck the gusher that made him a very rich man. He later started American Airlines, owned a professional sports team, and amassed the vast collection of art and antiques I'm now walking among.

His first fortune was made in drilling oil wells and it started with 92 consecutive dry holes. That is a lot of failure! I wonder on which dry hole most of us would have stopped trying?

Probably 10 or 11 for most of us.

Would we have made it to 40 … or maybe 56? Surely, very few of us would continue on to 75 … or past 90.

But Amon Carter kept drilling until he hit pay dirt and became instantly wealthy. Let me re-phrase that: There was nothing instant about his wealth and success. It was the result of much hard work, sacrifice, investment, and persistence.

There is that word again: persistence. It is the dogged determination to never give up. It is being gripped by the grit to stay with the job.

The resolve to not turn back until your goals are met. Call it persistence, determination, grit, gumption, or resolve, Amon Carter had it.

I wonder how many oilmen had the same goals and dreams as Carter. How many potential oil millionaires quit on number 92… just before success? They went to their graves still dreaming of that gusher while Amon Carter just kept drilling. I wonder how many more he would have drilled had number 93 also been dry?

Once again, I'm reminded that success in life is in large part simply refusing to quit, showing up every day, pushing, sweating, and working hard.

Persistence.

And its first cousin, perseverance.

The opposite of quitting. Amon Carter had it—this resolve, defined as "to act with determination…. steadfast and faithful."

A "lucky Texas oilman" who just wouldn't quit.

92 dry holes or not.

The following poem is by my beloved cousin, Mary V Iles Hudson. "Aunt Mary V" is one of the few remaining great-grandchildren of Joe and Eliza Moore, the heroes of *The Wayfaring Stranger* and *A Good Place.*

She is a wonderful writer and I'm so grateful for her allowing this inspiring poem to be included in *Deep Roots.*

Aunt Mary V's beautiful hands are holding the pine seedling on the back cover of this book.

Perseverance

A seed fell on a certain spot.
Just how or when mankind knows not.
It pushed through sod to hold its head up straight.
Then quietly, trusting nature seemed to wait
For sunshine, rain, and wind.
How could it know t'would bend?
There must have come a storm so great until
It grasped that tree with hands like steel
And bent it o'er against its will.
O lovely leaning tree!
Explain your mystery, your charm,
So all may hear!
T'is though a small still voice speaks,
"Persevere!"

Mary V. Iles Hudson

Running in the Lobby

30 seconds, 8 short minutes, 76 years ago

It's nearly midnight—Mountain Daylight Time on the last night of a Writers Conference. I'm sitting on the floor in the Marriott Denver lobby. I'm close to an electric plug for the laptop and can spread out my papers.

I'm doing what I love best: writing. It's quiet. Everyone with any sense has gone to bed.

I'm glad I'm up because if I hadn't been I'd missed them.

I heard them before I saw them: First I heard their giggling, then the sound of their steps. A young couple in white, hand in hand, sprinting through the lobby. She wore a beautiful wedding dress, carrying her slippers in one hand. The groom wore a matching white tuxedo as he hollered a Rocky Mountain version of the Rebel Yell.

They were running (as much as you can run in a wedding dress) toward the elevator. Visibly deeply in love. Laughing. Full of emotion from a special day that'll live on in their hearts.

They didn't see me behind a potted palm, but I couldn't resist, "Congratulations." They waved while impatiently waiting at the elevator. I added, "My wife and I just celebrated thirty years. Believe me, it only gets better."

The bride smiled. "Then congratulations to you." The elevator opened, and they were gone. The whole scene probably took thirty seconds.

I only saw them for that brief moment in time. My prayer is that they'll feel the same way in thirty years that DeDe and I do.

I thought back to that Thursday—August 9, 1979. We

were married in her parents' living room. I have a photo of us as a newly married couple with the mantel clock behind us. It reads 2:08 PM.

Our wedding took eight minutes. However, a knot can be definitely tied securely in less than eight minutes. It's a matter of the heart.

Eight minutes. Thirty years ago on an August afternoon. Brought back to my memory a running giggling newlywed couple in the lobby of the Denver Marriott.

The young couple in the lobby made me think about Uncle Gordon and Aunt Letha. They don't run across lobbies anymore. Their mode of travel are matching wheelchairs at the Kinder Nursing Home.

Aunt Letha is my paternal grandmother's sister and Uncle Gordon is her loving spouse of seventy-six years.

Last year, Uncle Gordon told me of their marriage day. "It was December 1932 when we eloped. Due to the nosy neighbors, we avoided the Oberlin courthouse. Our arrival in Lake Charles brought an unpleasant surprise—a long line of couples snaked out of the Clerk of Court's office. Texas had more stringent laws on marrying and most of the waiting couples had crossed the Sabine to get 'married quickly'."

With a sparkle in his eye, he continued, "I'm sure folks thought we wouldn't last, but they were wrong." He stared across the room they shared at the Kinder Nursing Home. "We're still together seventy-six years later."

I was always amazed how their mannerisms and speech were so similar. I guess three-quarters of a century living together welds two hearts, lives, and even personalities into one. To me they modeled grace and commitment. They didn't have to talk about the strength of their marriage. It showed in every action and deed.

In the "lowlands" of temporary things and throwaway relationships, the towering marriage of Gordon and Letha Reynolds looms as Mt. Everest.

A marriage where two became one.

A joyful marriage where "unto death do us part" took seventy-six years to come.

When Aunt Letha died last September, everyone worried about Uncle Gordon. He was 98 and now alone—separated from his mate. How would he react to that first anniversary—December 25—spent apart?

After seventy-six Christmas Days as man and wife, he would be alone on this one, but their separation was short-lived. Uncle Gordon followed quickly behind his wife, dying just days before Christmas.

I believe they were back together for their 77th anniversary—with many more to come.

Thanks Uncle Gordon and Aunt Letha for showing us how it's done.

Seventy-six years.

Even eight short minutes thirty long years ago.

Then a thirty-second encounter in a Denver Hotel lobby.

It's all about a thing called love.

Long live love.

Le Petit Baton Rouge

The strong smell of hot peppers and vinegar stings your eyes and nostrils when arriving at Avery Island, Louisiana.

You're at the home of Tabasco Hot Sauce, south of Lafayette, Louisiana.

Avery Island is not an actual island. It is a rounded hill rising above the surrounding flat marsh. Its elevation is due to the underground salt dome beneath the "island."

This salt dome led to development of the world's most famous hot sauce. Salt is one the three major ingredients in Tabasco; the other two are vinegar and red peppers.

Home of numerous waterfowl species, hundreds of alligators, and beautiful plant life, Avery Island is a must-see destination for visitors to our diverse state. In addition to the flora and fauna of "The Island," no trip is complete without touring the Tabasco plant.

A tour of the facility reveals how the ingredients are harvested and mixed. In the showroom, hundreds of Tabasco products are displayed in every size and type imaginable.

Rows of the tiny two-inch-long Tabasco bottles are arranged liked soldiers awaiting the order to charge. These mini-bottles are included in every "Meal Ready to Eat" used by the military.

These military meals are commonly called "M.R.E.'s" and they contain various entrees, condiments, and drink mixes, as well as a bottle of Tabasco.

On a recent trip to Ethiopia, I saw these small Tabasco bottles for sale in the markets. An Ethiopian friend said, "Those bottles came from the M.R.E.'s supplied by your government after our recent famine. Not knowing what Tabasco is, and not able to read English, they were originally sold in the markets as 'women's perfume'."

We laughed as I envisioned an Ethiopian wife applying Tabasco to her neck in anticipation of a romantic evening. I then told my African friend of the name we call the M.R.E.'s: "Meals Rejected by Ethiopians."

A few years ago while touring the Tabasco plant at Avery Island, I saw the little red stick, or "le petit baton rouge" as it is called in French. Every Tabasco pepper picker carries one in his or her hand.

During the harvest, each worker holds the the red stick beside each pepper, ensuring the correct ripeness. This comparison process between the painted stick and the pepper results in the consistent taste of Tabasco sauce enjoyed the world over.

This stick, painted this very particular shade of red, is used as the standard for picking. The pickers carefully compare the fruit on the bush with the red stick. Only those with the correct coloration are picked—not green, not orange. Just the perfect red.

Here's a neat application to "le petit baton rouge." As the world looks at the followers of Jesus, they are looking for a difference in our lives that is caused by our Savior. They are not as interested in our churches, music, and preaching as they are in seeing this difference.

Here is what they are looking for: It's a simple word called love. As folks look at our lives, they will compare us to the teachings and love of Jesus. In other words, they compare our fruit against the "le petit baton rouge" of the teachings of Jesus.

Jesus very clearly emphasized the defining mark (or color) of a Christian in John 13:34-35, "A new command I give you: Love one another. As I have loved you, so you must love one another. By this all men will know that you are my disciples, if you love one another."

There it is: the fruit of my life as a follower of Jesus

should be the color of love. A love that begins by loving those around me as in "Love one another . . . "

But it's also a love that refuses to stay indoors among its own kind. This "Jesus-kind of love" flows out in a ripple effect where lives are changed and enriched. Others are watching. They are using their petit baton rouges in judging and comparing our lives. But here's the scary part: Jesus himself, the living Son of God, is also applying his red stick against our lives.

We can never come close in meeting his standard. He was perfect, is perfect, and will always be perfect. However, by growing closer and closer to Jesus… we will take on "His Color."

… And His Color is always love. His "petit baton rouge" was not really petit (or little.) It was large—a large wooden cross—an instrument of death. And just like the Avery Island stick, it was dipped in red. The blood on that cross was from the very Son of God.

And here is the best part: He willingly went to that cross personally for you … willingly paying for your sins. What will you personally do about that?

A person has two simple choices: Embrace that love-gift of Jesus and commit your life and heart to Him personally… or walk by it rejecting the chance to be in relationship with the very Son of God.

It's your choice. You hold the decision in your hand.

Or rather in your heart.

Here I am! I stand at the door and knock. If anyone hears my voice and opens the door, I will come in and eat with him, and he with me.
Revelation 3:20

Wings and Roots

If asked what I like best about purple martins, I'll reply, "It's how these birds have wings and roots.

One of the joys of my rural life is the six months the martins spend as my guests. These migratory birds, members of the swallow family, first arrive in Louisiana in February. Two months later, they begin building nests, and by June, the first eggs hatch. The baby birds are flying by July, and the entire colony will be gone by August.

When you understand their history and habits, you'll grasp why I love them. Long before my ancestors came to Louisiana, Native Americans had colonized them after discovering how they devoured mosquitoes by the thousands. The Indians hung birdhouses made from dried gourds attracting these birds, which seemed to prefer living near humans.

Early pioneers also adopted these birds, and martin boxes and gourds were common around early dwellings. This love affair between humans and martins has continued as people expectantly await their arrival each spring.

If you ask most martin landlords what they love best about the birds, the answer is usually, "Their singing is beautiful."

It's hard to describe their song. I've heard it said in so many ways:

"A bubbling sound going up and down."

"A happy song."

"They sing as they gargle creek water and grit their teeth," was how one older woman explained it.

Regardless of the description, it's a song to love. Coming outside on a spring morning and hearing their playful singing,

I'm happy knowing they've paid me the honor of spending part of the year with my family.

The hatched babies quickly grow, "feather up," and are soon making their first tentative flights. Last year, during this time when the young are very susceptible to predators, I found a squawking baby on the ground. Before our cat could find it, I scooped the trembling bird up. .

Opening my hands, I tossed the young bird into the air. It struggled and flew a short distance. Chasing it down, I caught the bird and tossed it again into the air. This time it flew much further before landing among high grass in our field. I left it there, hoping for the best.

That is when I thought about my youngest son, Terry.

Just as I've tossed the martin in the air, Terry's mother and I are doing the same for him. He's leaving in a few weeks for a summer in South Asia. He'll be hiking along the historic rivers and foothills of the Himalayas in this remote and fascinating part of the world.

We trust the Lord, as well as this young man we've raised. From my own Asian trips, I've learned you never come back the same. Seeing the vast world and its great poverty changes Americans—as it should.

I know he will come back different—stronger, wiser, and looking at his own world differently.

He'll even look differently at the Wal-Mart pet food aisle. Walking among real poverty and hunger puts into perspective how many of our animals eat better than these needy people.

Terry will feel that too. Just like my new flying birds, he's going on a long journey from which one never returns to earth quite the same.

As June drifts by, all of the young birds leave the nest. The sky is now filled with martins as the young birds join their parents in flight. They soar in the wind, and it is obvious they're enjoying doing what they were born to do.

Watching their flight, I understand why men in earlier times attempted to build flying machines. We humans are always subconsciously jealous when we see a soaring bird. King David's words in Psalms 55 express this, "Oh, that I had wings of a dove! I would fly away and be at rest."

Watching these martins fly, the sad thought hits me as to how soon they'll be gone. One morning, probably within a month, I'll walk outside to enjoy their singing and flying, only to find the sky is silent, and my birds gone.

I recall the previous February when the first two martin scouts arrived on a cold rainy day. I was surprised seeing them this early in such bad weather. The pair stayed throughout the day huddled on the box ledge. Then, as abruptly as they had appeared, they were gone.

I knew eventually I'd see them again. Sure enough, within a week they were back with their entire colony.

Martins spend their winters in Brazil, nesting in hollow trees and living among the great expanse of the Amazon jungle. Sometime after the first of the year, when their instincts tell them, they begin flying northward in small groups.

Ornithologists believe they fly in groups of three or four to avoid entire colonies being wiped out in storms over the Gulf of Mexico. When they finally reach land, they regroup into large flocks near bodies of fresh water, replenishing and resting after this exhausting flight.

Shortly after grouping up in these huge colonies along the southern coast, the martin scouts head back to the exact site of the previous year's nesting, which is the place of birth for most of the colony.

To me, the marvelous instinct possessed by these birds is a clear indication of a Master Designer. I always think of their Creator, when these birds faithfully return to their home in my yard. The words of my grandfather echo, "It'd be hard to study birds and be an atheist."

Watching their yearly arrival, I'm reminded how these birds have both wings and roots.

Wings carrying them on a long round trip journey past the equator and back, and roots bringing them home—unerringly each spring to the same box in my yard from which they were hatched.

Wings and roots. Two things that are good to have.

These are two things I've tried giving each of my older boys. It's something I'm trying to instill in Terry as he begins his journey nearly halfway around the world.

I compare the two trips mileage-wise: Terry's journey will cover about eight thousand miles. It's ironic that some martins, those commuting from Brazil to their extreme breeding range in Southern Canada, will travel about the same distance—eight thousand miles of flight.

Later in the year, watching the martins, I think about their long upcoming journey. Each day, they spend less time around the bird boxes. The adult martins take the juveniles on longer flights in preparation for the challenging journey ahead. As each day's flights lengthen, it is clear that soon I'll walk outside one morning to find the singing I love so much gone.

I'm happily enjoying another year with these friends. I remind myself they are doing what they were born to do—leaving the nest flying high and far. Even though I'd like to keep them year round, I'd never deny them the freedom of their long adventure across the ocean between two continents.

Pondering how quiet it will be when these birds are gone, I think about how each of our boys did what children are supposed to do—they grew up and left home. Terry is the latest—and last one to do this. Only yesterday, he was small—just learning to fly—as I taught him how to stand in the batter's box.

Now he is a six-foot-four inch grown man seemingly flying on his own. He's a long ways from that eight-year-old who proudly announced his life's goal: "I'm going to grow up and play for the Houston Astros—or drive a Little Debbie's truck."

Once again, I hear the song of the martins as the young birds learn the joy of soaring and diving. Then, I see—this time in my mind—the young martins, silhouetted against the sky, making their first long journey across the ocean. Through both clear blue skies, as well as in the midst of storms, they fly on, guided by the stars and the instinctive internal compass God has placed within their tiny bodies.

Crossing the vast ocean through a strong wind mixed with fog and rain, the young martins near exhaustion, ready to fall from the sky. One of the mature birds, a long-time veteran of this trip, flies nearer and silently wills the young birds to continue on. Then through a break in the clouds, the coast of South America looms below. They've made it—their first trip to their winter home.

Thinking of Terry—and where he is headed, I'm reminded that the best, happiest, and safest place to be is in the center of God's will. This is all I can ask from God—for Him to lead my son into this special place in His will, wherever that may be.

Finally, one last time before going inside, I watch the younger martins gathered on the electrical line, readying for their big flight.

Just as I would never stop these birds from going where God, through instinct, has sent them, I know I would not stop my son, or any of the special young people I know and love, from their journey in finding God's will for their lives.

It's nearly dark now and walking back inside the house, I'm happy—knowing that at least for today, I have my martins—and son—to enjoy being with.

I'm happy they have wings,
and just as happy they have deep roots.

Dead End

Mr. Frank Miller stormed into my office. Maybe stormed is too strong a word, but he was evidently highly upset. When a man over eighty rushes into a room, one quickly wants to find out what's wrong. Mr. Frank got right to the point. "Curt, have you been to the cemetery?"

"No sir, at least not this week. What's wrong?"

In my mind, I imagined desecrated graves or some such vandalism.

"So you haven't heard—or seen—the sign the police jury has put up?"

"No sir, but—"

Mr. Frank was too upset to let me finish. "Right where you turn off to the cemetery, they've put up a sign that reads, 'Dead End'."

"What?"

"Dead End! They've put up a sign going to the cemetery that says 'Dead End.' We'll be the laughing stock of the whole world when word gets out."

Now reader, I know you are laughing right now. I would have laughed also if I hadn't known that Mr. Frank was 'dead serious' about the sign.

He continued as I tried suppressing the giggles that were spurting loose inside me. "We need to call a board meeting and do something about it. It's unacceptable. It shows a serious lack of respect for our cemetery."

With that, he whirled on his heel and marched out, evidently to gather a lynch mob to go to the police juror office in DeRidder.

When he left, I quickly closed my door, sat down, and laughed until I hurt.

Then I did the next logical thing—I got in my truck and drove to the cemetery. There it was at the turnoff, just past the road sign that directed drivers to Dry Creek Cemetery.

Dead End.

I had another good laugh.

The next day, Mr. Frank paid a return visit. He was much calmer this time because he had a plan. "Curt, I've thought a lot about that sign. You do remember it, don't you?"

"Oh yes sir, Mr. Frank. I went to see it for myself." I hoped I wasn't smiling.

"I've given it some serious thought. We can compromise with the police juror. We'll get them to replace the dead end sign with one entitled, Cul-de-sac."

I was confused. "What?"

"Cul-de-sac."

He spelled it. "C-u-l d-e s-a-c." Then he smiled. "It's French for dead end."

I knew what a cul-de-sac was—it's those circle driveways in cities where rich people live.

I should not have said it, but I did. "But, Mr. Frank, most people in Dry Creek will have no idea what a cul-de-sac is. I believe it will cause more confusion than there is now."

He stammered, "But that would be a heck of a lot better than the dead end sign."

I realized I'd probably hurt his feelings with my lack of enthusiasm for the cul-de-sac sign. I assured him we would get the sign removed and leave it at that.

However, before the road crew could remove the sign, it disappeared on its own. It was gone—post and all. And no one knew what had happened.

I could just see this old man driving to the cemetery turnoff late at night with his headlights off, getting out, and pulling up the sign.

The sign was nowhere to be found, and no one said a

word. I respected Mr. Frank too much to accuse him of this act.

He never mentioned the dead end sign again. The year after the sign's disappearance, Mr. Frank died from a stroke.

His Dry Creek funeral was one of the finest I've ever attended. I always thought he would have enjoyed the stories and memories that were shared.

I was one of the pallbearers. As we drove to the cemetery in the long procession of vehicles, I smiled as we passed the spot where the dead end sign had been.

It was gone. Tears came to my eyes, as I thought about how much I would miss my special friend. At the same time, I felt warm inside as I cherished all of the stories, memories, advice, and mentoring given me by this memorable man.

Then a thought came to me. A thought I believe was from the Lord. There is no "dead end sign" on the cemetery road for the believer in Jesus. The Savior's very words at another cemetery are clear, "I am the resurrection and the life. He who believes in me will live again. I am the resurrection and the life; he who believes in me shall never die. Do you believe this?"

I quietly said, "Yes."

For the believer, it is not a dead end, but a new beginning.

Postscript

About two years after Mr. Frank Miller's death, one of his grandsons, relatively sure that the statute of limitations had run out, said, "Mr. Curt, you remember that black and yellow dead end sign Pa hated so bad?"

"Sure, I remember it."

"Well, I know where it is. Pa had me and David go pull it up one night and throw it in Little Dry Creek—and that's where it's still at."

As I said, there's no dead end sign on the road to the cemetery.

ஐ

It is only appropriate that this book called *Deep Roots*

ends with a story entitled, "Dead End."

This is the last story in the book, but it is not the end. I've found that a book of short stories—especially stories of the heart—never ends. Readers, like you, will take the stories and retell them, adding their own personal touches and prompting them to tell new stories.

That is good.

There is no dead end with stories. They outlive our telling.

And that's a good thing.

Epilogue: Why I Write:

"If you're able to quit writing, you probably should." -Cec Murphey

I write for the simple joy of expression. I have fifty-one journals that I've filled with stories, dreams, ideas, and the journey of my life since age seventeen.

If I never published another single word, I'd still write. It's what I do. I guess it's who I am. I have one final story that expresses the reason that I publish and share my writing:

The man's voice was so soft that I shifted the telephone receiver to hear better. "Sir, you don't know me, but I've read your book."

He sounded older than me, and I was struck by the strange blend of sadness and calmness in his words. "I read your book in Angola Prison."

He had my full attention. "Which book?"

"Stories from the Creekbank."

"How'd you get my book in Angola?"

"I don't know how it got there, but God used it to change my life."

I listened carefully. In spite of being a speaker, I had nothing to say.

"I made a promise that when I was released, I'd call and thank you. I'm keeping that promise."

I'm ashamed to say I didn't get his name. I was too touched to respond.

That was four years ago. I'd just started writing and speaking full time and had inner doubts if we'd make it. The gift of his call was what I needed to move forward and take any risks needed to write, share, and grow.

I write for the two "I" words: Influence and Impact. I want my words to have a wide ripple effect of influence. I want them to travel to places I've never been.

Like Angola Prison, or maybe Angola, Africa.

I wish for my writing to have a deep-rooted reverberation into the hearts of readers. That's impact.

I've thought about my Angola friend's call many times. A humorous critic told me, "I know how your book got to Angola. Someone gave it to Goodwill." He added with a wink. "One man's trash is another man's treasure."

He's right—I have another faithful reader in Colfax that first "discovered" my books on top of a dumpster at the Grant Parish Landfill.

Where will this book that you're holding travel to?

I hope it first lingers in your heart. I wish for impact and encouragement for you. Who knows where it will go next? Feel free to keep it and re-read it over the years. But you have permission to pass it on if you're finished with it. Share it with a friend . . . or send it to Goodwill.

Who knows where it'll end up?

Like the fluttering pine seeds that helicopter-down from the cones, our words—written or spoken—can travel on the wind far beyond where we are rooted.

We never know where they'll take hold, sprout, and reach downward into fertile soil.

That's why we call it deep roots.

Still digging, still growing,
Curt Iles

Information for Book Clubs is available by visiting our website at www.creekbank.net

Other titles by the author:

Stories from the Creekbank (2000)

The Old House (2002)

Wind in the Pines (2004)

Hearts across the Water (2005)

The Mockingbird's Song (2007)

The Wayfaring Stranger (2007)

A Good Place (2009)

Deep Roots (2010)

Available on audio CDs: “Wind in the Pines,” “Hearts across the Water,” and “Front Porch Stories”

To order:
$15.00 per copy plus $5.00 shipping per order.
Visit our bookstore at www.creekbank.net for complete ordering information.

Contact information:
Creekbank Stories
PO Box 332
Dry Creek, LA 70637
Toll free 1(866) 520-1947
(337) 328-7215

Curt Iles writes from his hometown of Dry Creek, Louisiana. An eighth-generation resident of western Louisiana's "No Man's Land", he is a storyteller who loves educating, entertaining, and inspiring through his writing and speaking. His life mission is to be a man God can use and have the respect of his wife, sons, and their families.

Curt and his wife DeDe are the parents of three sons and five grandchildren. They enjoy traveling to Africa, mentoring young people, and celebrating life in Louisiana's Piney Woods.

He is shown above with his mother, Mary Iles. The painting in the background, "Doten at the Old House" is by his uncle, Bill Iles. It features Curt's great-grandmother, Theodosia Wagnon Iles and the family's "Old House."

Learn more at www.creekbank.net
Creekbank Stories
PO Box 332
Dry Creek, LA 70637
Toll free 1.866.520.1947

For corrections, input, and suggestions,
email us at curtiles@aol.com
www.creekbank.net
Join us at Face book and Twitter

Curt is represented by Terry Burns of Hartline Agency.
www. www.hartlineliterary.com

Creekbank Stories has a simple goal: to connect hearts to God through inspiring stories. To learn more about our writing and speaking, contact us at www.creekbank.net